Asleep in Coronation Market

BARRINGTON WRIGHT

Library of Congress Control Number   APPLIED
ISBN   Softcover   978-1-950955-32-9
              Hardcover   978-1-950955-33-6
              Ebook   978-1-950955-34-3

Printed in the United States of America.

Book Vine Press
2516 Highland Dr.
Palatine, IL 60067

SUGGESTED AUDIENCE

"Readers of *Asleep in Coronation Market* will include people native to the Caribbean and people with backgrounds in other parts of the world. They will be stimulated to think about the underlying issues; some local, others universal; some contemporary, others historical. They will be reminded of dehumanizing instrumentality of society's under class and gain insight into the universal dilemma of typical poor mothers' unequal family burden. Like Virginia, such mothers travel to foreign countries in search of financial opportunities, but reap intolerable hardships. Including unintended consequences of their children's descent into perilous depths of despair because of anxieties associated with parental separation. But readers will also find comic relief in the setting, the dialogue, and the characters' sense of humor. Hopefully they will cheerfully support the main character's positive response to the discovery of stimulating friendships."

UNA TAPPER, ESQ.

ACKNOWLEDGEMENTS

This story of a misguided young man sleep-walking in Coronation Market had a long incubation period, until I shared my thoughts about the character during a New Year's Eve celebration. Thanks to my friends, John Howard, John Kavanaugh, Joan Kavanaugh, Keren Leahy, Robbie Paterson, and Tedde Tasheff. They encouraged me to write the story, share periodic updates with the group, in exchange for their feedback on the information about Jamaican cultural norms and the enduring legacy of its unmatched tropical beaches during that period. Thanks to my long-standing high school friend, Judith Nembhard, who read portions of the earliest draft and whose questions about Point of View demanded answers that improved the coherence of the narrative. Thanks also to LaSonya Thompson who challenged me to develop a writing schedule in support of my efforts to complete the novel.

CONTENTS

CHAPTER 1

Hope Meets Despair in Coronation Market

Harry no longer wanted to answer questions about the whereabouts of his mother, Virginia. But when he did, he answered curtly, "I don't know!" Many times, his answer offended the more inquisitive neighbors who redoubled their efforts with follow-up questions. By contrast, less inquisitive neighbors who perceived his reluctance to speak about his mother, avoided all interactions with him. The unwanted questions from some neighbors and punishing silence by others contributed to his self-imposed isolation and his struggles to answer his own questions about his mother. Why has she not contacted him since she left home? Has she abandoned him? What misfortunes has she suffered? Is she dead? Her absence created a void in his life and the life of his great-grandfather, Tarta. In her absence, activities in the household slowed to a sloth's crawl. No more coconut oil production, no more purchase and sale of bananas, no hiring of local workers. Those workers no longer had jobs. The cultivated ground provisions Tarta brought home from the field to feed himself and Harry were more than they needed, but Tarta was less resourceful than Virginia in selling the excess. The family became cash poor. The cooking deteriorated. The home attracted very few visitors for friendly visits or a meal.

Each day of Harry's experience was a step by step journey into despair. He lost interest in elementary school and skipped classes frequently, but Tarta was not alert enough to realize it or correct his behavior. Harry left the house for school each day, but went to a favorite location at the beach to daydream. He found an abandoned hammock in a tree that hugged him during his escape from home, school, and everyone. He found solace listening to the sound of waves rushing to the shore, and the gentle sea breeze whistling through the trees in harmony with a variety of birdsongs. He spent many hours looking up in the sky. He saw carefree birds, including black John Crows with distinguishing red head and outstretched wings flying effortlessly over land and sea. They were a fitting contrast to the white pelicans hovering high above the sea until they identified a school of fish to prey on. Without warning and with lightning speed, a pelican plunged into the sea and emerged with a fish partly hanging from its bill. Sometimes Harry witnessed the pelicans with the catch being outmaneuvered and losing its meal to more opportunistic competitors. He had fun inventing the nickname, Winged Buccaneers, for the predatory birds. It was his way of mocking their human counterpart, Henry Morgan, the British Buccaneer whom his teachers said plundered Spanish vessels from his base in Jamaica, during the 17th century.

Harry broke the monotony of the hammock some afternoons when he summoned enough energy to assist fishermen haul their seine from the sea with the day's catch. He also enjoyed listening to their exploits at sea. He did not have to avoid those men, because no one asked him about his mother. At the end of their interactions, the men rewarded him with small donations, referred to as pocket money.

After hanging around the beach for a while, he decided on a plan to avoid the experience of losing Tarta, his last surviving relative. His ingenious plan would have him leaving Tarta before Tarta left him. He was determined not to wait for death to separate them. His separation would leave them alive. He would disappear like both his father and mother, but he would not be gone forever like Mammy, his great-grandmother. He would hang around Coronation Market, the highlight of his mother's business activities, until he connected with her spirit.

He secretly left home one night for Coronation Market. But he did not fully anticipate the experience of travelling for the first time without his mother at night on a truck full of higglers with loads of food stuff to be sold in Kingston Coronation Market. It was about 8:00 PM, on a Wednesday night, when he hopped on the back of the roofless truck after sidemen loaded the goods, closed the flip down back door and made sure that all higglers were safely seated. After the sidemen returned to the cab with the driver, Harry clung to the closed back door of the truck with both hands as the truck began to drive away. The driver could not see him in the rearview mirror. He ran behind the truck in that hidden position for a short distance before the truck gained speed. When he gathered enough momentum, he leaped unto the truck then climbed over the back door into the truck. It would take him another minute to shuffle himself between the paying passengers and their goods. Every breath he took was filled with the smell of crocus bags, breadfruit, yams, coconuts, bananas, and sweat. In mark contrast to other passengers, he was travelling light. With no possessions but the clothes he was wearing, he felt more secure hiding among marketable products. He knew that passengers on the truck had to pay the driver for the ride at the end of their destination in Kingston, but he had various concerns about the consequences of his inability to pay the fare, before or after he arrived at his destination. First, if the driver followed normal practice to avoid overload penalties before encountering police at unpredictable checkpoints along the road, he would stop the truck, have the sideman verify the last count to ensure that the truck was not overloaded with passengers. Second, the driver could stop at the most isolated area along the country road and discovered that Harry boarded the truck after the last count? He would calculate the fare from where Harry boarded, then demand immediate payment."

Harry worried that without money to pay his fare, the driver would force him off the truck and leave him in darkness on the most treacherous portion of the highway. He was so terrified by that possibility, that he prayed silently for God's protection all the way to

Kingston. He believed God answered his prayer. He jumped off the truck without being seen by the driver, during a traffic jam on West Street, a short distance from the market.

He walked to the market with his empty hands. He was not a higgler. He had nothing to sell. In his mind, he was worth less than the perishable goods in crocus bags. Even worse, he had no money to buy food. He had embarked on a survival strategy that avoided what he saw soldier crabs and turtles doing while he was hanging out at the beach. They walked around with their shell houses as permanent protection of their bodies from external threats. But their protection slowed their movements to a crawl. They couldn't travel fast, even in emergencies. With those examples in his mind, he decided on a plan with more flexibility. His plan would free his body from encumbrances, while optimizing his physical and mental agility. Most importantly, with his wide-open mind, nothing would interfere with his ability to reconnect with his mother.

At Coronation Market, he located the spot where his mother often sold coconut oil and bananas. It was not a stall. It was just a rented spot in front of a stall. Someone else was now occupying her spot. He stood there for a long time, often brushed aside by the tide of people hurrying to purchase items. At midnight, when the Market closed, he was locked in with higglers who had not sold all their products. He mimicked the scavenging goats, rats, and carrion birds that fed on the garbage thrown over the eastern fence of the market during the night. But before sanitation workers removed the garbage, Harry would compete with flies and maggots, the first claimants of discarded fruits, and chose those that were at least 10 percent edible. To avoid the maggots, he developed a keen sense of touch and used his fingers to identify and discard the most putrid portion of the fruits. He then nibbled around rotting portions of mangoes, bananas, jackfruits, star apples, and other fruits. Sometimes he supplemented his fruit diet with stale bread, after discarding the portions covered with green molds. His difficulty in feeding himself was matched by the uncomfortable places he slept. After a while, he became so tired that he could sleep while standing rather than falling asleep. He even progressed to sleep while walking, during the day or night. Eventually, many higglers did not want to see him near their stalls. They were convinced that his presence near their stall was bad luck. If he did not get out of their way fast enough, they would push him away and call the market police to banish him from the market. He did not resent what they were doing to his body, which was his living sacrifice to efforts of reuniting his mother's spirit with his.

The hardships of finding food was only surpassed by where to excrete the little he had eaten. There were no public toilets. The streets were too busy and not dark enough for him to empty his body's waste on the street. So, one night before the market closed, he walked down Darling Street toward the train station. On the way, a lignum vitae tree beckoned him with its inviting branches. He accepted the invitation and climbed to a place comfortable enough to rest and sleep. Most importantly, he could relieve himself at nights without anyone seeing him. It was up to people to watch their steps while walking on Darling Street.

Within a few months Harry literally wore out the only clothes he possessed. He had been wearing the same filthy clothes every day since he arrived at the Market. Those clothes complemented the apparent neglect of his body. Dirt and sweat in the tropical heat harmonized to produce a repulsive odor that signaled his arrival to everyone he encountered. Weakness in the seat of his pants and the armpits of his shirt gave way to gaping holes, after repeated heavy downpour of rain. Additionally, some higglers doused him with dirty waste water to punish him for his filthy appearance. Before long, his clothes refused to endure such predictable assaults each day and abandoned him while he walked about naked in plain view of every-one. But his unsightly appearance was of little concern to busy shop-pers in the market. He might even have been invisible to most of them, if his odoriferous presence were not such a nuisance. He was in Coronation Market, not the Garden of Eden. He was naked without fig leaves and no one to cover his nakedness.

One afternoon, two girls wearing school uniforms of white blouses and pleated navy-blue skirts, saw Harry sleepwalking. One girl said to the other, "Look at that man walking in his sleep. That's the condition Ms. Brown was talking about in class today. The name she called it was 'sam-nam-bolis.'"

The other girl laughed before offering her correction. "The word is 'som'nambulist.' You pronounced it with the emphasis in the wrong place. You made the word sound like a person named Sam, ate something called bolis. The emphasis should be on the first syllable 'som,' not the second syllable, 'nam.'"

They were also laughing for other reasons that had nothing to do with his sleepwalking. He was totally exposed and well-endowed, and they were amused by his pendulum swinging between his legs when he walked.

One morning, while Harry was still perched on the lignum vitae tree, two boys in khaki school uniforms threw stones at targeted flowers on the tree branches. Some stones missed their targets, but came close to hitting Harry. When the boys eventually saw Harry, his presence surprised them. One boy mockingly called out to the other boy, "Jerry, look at the human sloth living in the lignum vitae tree. His whole body is covered with hair. I wonder how he sleeps without falling off the tree? Maybe he clung to the tree with his fingernails that may have grown into claws."

When Harry heard the word sloth, he immediately remembered his mother's prayer, that God should turn him into a sloth. But the boys' discussion of the animal's behavior shed new light on the reality of his mother's request. He learned that sloth was a tropical animal that slept in trees. It was slow, lazy, and infested with insects that lived on its hairy body. The name sloth was a nickname for laziness, one of the seven deadly sins in the Bible. With that new knowledge, Harry had a few questions for God, "Why did you answer my mother's prayer, if you knew it was a curse? Why should a five-year-old child be eternally cursed for trying to play with chickens in the kitchen at dinnertime? What if my mother heard the word sloth during a sermon at church and did not fully understand the effects of such a curse? Why didn't you, God, enlighten her before answering her prayer?" He even wondered if God were white, because Tarta explained how cruel white people were to Black people from Africa.

While listening to the boys he almost lost his balance on the tree. But his physical unsteadiness did not dislodge memories of Tarta's stories, and they popped back into his head as the boys walked away. "Mental slavery has no visible chains. It is in people's heads rather on their hands and feet. It's harder to break. A smart Maroon like you will find out how to break those chains, when you understand that it has to be broken from within you, rather than from the outside."

Suddenly, Harry's mind became a big lantern in a dark room, and he began to see the invisible chains that bound him to Coronation Market, Darling Street, and the lignum vitae tree. He started the downside up journey, by climbing down from the tree, just when two Rasta men were walking by. One shouted, "Rhaatid! Breda Zacchaeus a climb down from the tree. You can't say him naked like a newborn baby, because him hairy-hairy. But him no have on a stitch of clothes."

The older Rasta man said to Harry, "Breda man, what is your name?" It took Harry a while to respond, partly because he was carefully climbing down from the tree and partly because he was shocked to hear someone speaking to him rather than swearing at him. Both men waited for his answer.

"Mi name Harry," he replied.

The younger man with the dreadlocks asked a follow-up question, "So where do you live, Harry?"

Harry quickly responded, "Nowhere."

With disdain, the man said, "Nowhere is not a place to live, but the Good Book never lies. It said, 'foxes have holes, birds have nests, but the son of man has no place to lay his weary head.' Di Book go on to say, 'the cattle on a thousand hills belong to I.' Everything belongs to I, not to the white man or the uptown people. So, mi a go get some clothes fi cover your nakedness. You stay rite here wid Ras Joshua. Mi will also get some food. Mi soon come back."

After he left, Ras Joshua said, "Barracuda is a righteous man in this modern Babylon. He believes in taking back what the rich has stolen and return it to the poor, because rich people are parasites. Dem just like love-bush on trees or ticks on cows. Dem suck di life from their host, moving from one cow to another or one tree to another. That is the Babylonian corruption of the Almighty's plan. Jah's plan is the one you see in the pasture, where little black birds carefully pick ticks off a cow's back, because the cow tail not long enough to swat the ticks away. Both the cow and the birds benefit from the relationship. No more tix biting the cow inna him back where the tail can't reach to swat it away. The little black birds fill them craw with ticks without harming the cow. The cow is happy. The black bird is happy. That's Almighty Jah's plan for the world. One hand washes the other, so to speak."

When Barracuda returned, he brought Harry two pairs of pants, two pairs of underpants, two shirts, and a pair of sandals. He showed them to Harry and said, "You don't need no more clothes than this. The Good Book said, 'Sufficient onto the day is the evil thereof.' That means, no need to store up riches for tomorrow. It also said we must welcome the Prodigal Son with a feast. So, we ago down to the rail yard where we make our abode. We will cut some Aloe Vera that grows wild in the train yard and you can use the juice to lather yourself. It will kill lice and any insect on your body. It is better than soap. Use the hose attached to the standpipe to spray water all over your body, from head to foot. After you clean up yourself we will have a feast, but there will be no Biblical fatted calf. Our meal will be vegetable Ital stew, couple of roasted breadfruits, and lemonade and juicy black mangoes for desert. The stew will include coconut milk, green beans, carrots, okra, onions, susumber, thyme, scotch bonnet peppers, and curry seeds. At the end of the meal, me and Ras Joshua will finalize the welcome event, relaxing with some weed in our chillum pipe. Let's go!"

The men lived in a shack made of discarded automobile parts and cardboard boxes. It offered minimal shelter, but no comfort. It was undoubtedly temporary, like soldier crab shell that could be easily discarded when necessary. They occasionally washed themselves with water from a hose attached to the standpipe a short distance from the shack. Their toilet was a distant patch of high grass that offered minimal privacy.

Harry washed himself, put on one set of the newly acquired clothes and sandals. But the bigger change was adjusting to speaking to other people, rather than being spoken about or rebuked. It had been a long time since he paid any attention to surrounding activities that did not relate to his quest to find his mother. So, he didn't know current events, had very little to say and worried about losing his anonymity. During the meal, Ras Joshua tried to engage Harry in familiar conversation. "Which parish you lived in before coming to Kingston?" The question implied that Harry was not a Kingston man. "I came from Manchester, and Barracuda came from Portland. He is from the East; I am from the West. We drifted into each other's path here in Kingston."

Harry started his reply by saying, "Before I answer your question, I say much respect to both of you, brethren, for your great kindness to me. You did not give me kindness in exchange for anything, because you could plainly see that mi no have nothing, not even clothes pon mi back or front. You picked me up, when everyone put me down or dash me weh like dutty garbage in a rubbish heap. So, me have a question fi you, why are you helping me?"

Joshua replied, "It is written in the Good Book that I must love you as Jah loves me. It's as simple as that."

Harry continued, "Although you have not asked me why I was walking about naked in the Market, I believe it is a question that I should try to answer. I arrive in Kingston with only the clothes I was wearing. Those clothes couldn't continue taking the wear and tear, so dem gave up on me little by little. Before you know it, I was half naked; but not long after, I was totally naked. At first, I was ashamed for people to see me half naked. But one day I heard two men talking about me. Other people who heard the discussion said they were university students. One of the men said I was crazy to be walking about half naked in public. The other said it was possible that I could be happily expressing my freedom. The shorter man laughed at the idea. But the taller one continued to explain my nakedness as freedom. He said a long time ago, some Greek people found out that they were happier when they had nothing physically or emotionally. They owned no houses, land, or substantial possessions. They were not in love with anyone, they were not angry with anyone, they did not miss anyone who died, they were not afraid of anyone, they were not involved in politics. The only thing they owned were a torn jacket, a staff, and a wallet. They lived in towns and got food by begging. They never even wore shoes. They believed that the true ruler is the person who wanted nothing. I was surprise that those Greek people were not called Grecian, like how people in Jamaica would be called Jamaicans. They were called Cynics."

While the men listened attentively, Harry continued, "When the last pieces of clothing fell apart and I was totally naked, it occurred to me that I was even more free than a Cynic because I was totally naked before everyone, without being ashamed. But unlike a Cynic, I had emotional ties to my mother and I missed her." He ended his statements by telling the men that the full story about his mother will have to wait for another day.

After Harry spoke, Barracuda said, "No wonder Babylon is falling down like London bridge. Young people are going to university to learn how to walk half naked on the street and couldn't care less about anybody but themselves."

Ras Joshua had a different opinion about nakedness. "The Good Book said God gave Adam and Eve a home in a beautiful garden called Eden. It had everything they needed, but the devil fooled them into believing that they could get wisdom by eating the forbidden fruit. To their surprise, they gained only self-consciousness and shame about their nakedness but no worthwhile knowledge, experience, or judgement. Neither the Cynics nor brother Harry invented nakedness. God intended us to be naked and not be ashamed. To this day all other animals but human beings walk about naked without any manifestation of shame. But it's also true that other male animals like the roosters, dogs, cows, and donkeys don't walk about with their dicks exposed. It appears that each of these animal's dick is an internal organ, hidden inside its body. The male voluntarily extends the dick when sexually aroused or otherwise necessary. Maybe Adam's dick was an internal organ like it is in other animals, before he ate the forbidden fruit. With his newfound wisdom he lost his voluntary ability to withdraw his dick from public view into his body. Eve saw Adam's dick for the first time and it reminded her of the serpent, so in shame they both decided to cover their private parts with fig leaves to hide from God. But the newly wise Adam and Eve didn't know that fig leaves couldn't hide them from God."

Barracuda was not satisfied with what he just heard from Ras Joshua. He challenged the idea that paradise was mainly about being naked. "Paradise was living in harmony with other people and with nature. Husband did not rule over wife, there was no pain in childbirth, the ground was not cursed, and people did not have to experience the sweat of hard labor every day of their lives until they died. But even though it became more difficult to live by the rules of nature, it is currently worse to live by the man-made rules of society, which are designed to benefit the rich and the powerful."

Ras Joshua ended the inquiry into Harry's background for the evening by saying, "Now that destiny has brought us together with brother Harry, we will do more than talking in the coming days."

Harry rested more comfortably that night than when he slept in the tree. He did not have to be afraid of falling. He was protected from rain showers. But his mind was not at rest, it was perplexed with mixed emotions. His mother's whereabouts haunted him. He still harbored the desire to find the answer to where she is. He felt grateful to the two men for giving him clothes, food, shelter, and time in conversation, even as he contemplated the meaning of Ras Joshua's statement: "We will do more than talking in the coming days."

Harry woke up at about 5:00 AM to the train yard activities outside the hut he and the brethren slept in. First, he heard the kachi alarm system, intended to call railway workers to the job, but loud enough to be heard by everyone in Kingston. Then he heard the noise of trains shunting from one track to another in preparation for the day's transport of people and products. Surprisingly, the noise of the train yard did not affect him while he slept in the tree a short distance away. His new friends also seemed to be unaffected by the noise. They were still sleeping, so he had more time to reflect on earlier discussions with them and with Tarta.

He reflected on Tarta's ideas that people are on a never-ending journey that started at birth and continued after death. That endless journey brought white people to Jamaica in search of something they could not find in their country. It led them to enslave Africans as well as Coolies from China and India. Maroons in Jamaica used the Myal ceremony to help their dead find a resting place. But a prevailing problem is helping the living to overcome the frustration of being hopelessly lost in various ways. First, they could be lost in a labyrinth of experiences, where instead of journeying to their central goal, they are lost in the distracting circles and squares that keep them away from the center. Second, they could be lost in a type of maze which has similarities to a labyrinth. But to be a little more confusing, it has not one, but many ways to get to the central goal. Third, people could be lost in a type of wilderness. Of the three, the wilderness is the most perplexing. There is no pathway to a goal or a way out. It is a wild place where people could become casualties of unanticipated incidents. People who survive the wilderness experiences are left with little more than unpleasant memories.

Tarta also believed that Jamaica had been a wilderness for Black people, brought to the island as slaves from Africa. Nanny helped some Maroons find a narrow path out of the wilderness when she killed some of those white oppressors. Unlike Nanny, Paul Bogle's experience in the wilderness ended tragically, when his opponents trapped him in a maze of man-made rules. They murdered him and the many people he was trying to help. But survivors in modern wilderness are still wandering with invisible chains. Many are frustrated to the point of surrendering to the temptation of no longer trying to reach their goals. Tarta felt that would be the biggest mistake. People must never give way to the feeling of defeat, because victory may be just around the corner.

Harry's friends woke up at about 7:00 AM and whipped up a quick breakfast of hot bush tea, white hard dough bread, and butter. During breakfast, Ras Joshua inquired where else in Kingston Harry travelled since he arrived in Coronation Market. He was not surprised to hear that Harry had only been to Darling Street and the train yard. He invited Harry to go with him to a street meeting at a place called Parade.

On the way to Parade, Joshua told Harry that there are similarities and important differences between Coronation Market and

Parade. "The place you have been living and where we are going are both markets. Coronation Market is a place where food stuff and other goods are exchanged for money. People in that market are either buying or selling something. But what is purchased must be as good or better than what someone else is selling at a different price. If you were not selling or buying anything when you were in that market, you were in the wrong place. You did not fit into the daily transactions that overlook spectators and ignore compassion. Even though some people may be kind, their compassion didn't fit into the purse they brought to the market. That purse opened to one choice—was that item worth the price? If it were not, they moved on without remorse. What happened in Coronation Market was like a cargo ship leaving England to buy bananas in Jamaica. The decision to buy does not consider how much labor was invested in planting, reaping, and transporting the bananas to the wharf. It was based on the facts that the bananas were fit, not bruised, had the required number of hands on the bunch and still edible after the rigors of transportation by sea. All that I have said adds up to this basic idea, if you don't have anything to sell or money to buy in Coronation Market, you may not even survive as a naked Cynic, because that market is not about ideas, it's about money exchanges for food products, the primary necessities of life. Unlike Coronation Market, Parade is a market of ideas, where food for thoughts is freely served. It reflects the saying in the Good Book: 'Man shall not live by bread alone, but by every word of God.' Parade divides east Kingston from west Kingston. Outside Parade, to the north, is a theatre; to the east and south are two big churches with huge bells always reminding people what time it is. But the daily market place of ideas occurs inside Parade, among various groups of promoters and followers. Marcus Garvey UNIA group is interested in restoring the dignity of Black people and the necessity of returning to Africa. Trade union groups including JLP and PNP are interested in higher wages and better working conditions for working-class people at the lowest end of society. Rastafarian group is interested in a budding religion, promoting Black people's centrality to the new Messiah, a God Man from Ethiopia. Various Christian groups are interested in going to heaven. Their leaders are promoting variations of the end times when the Messiah will soon come to redeem people who are saved. In addition to the rich menu of ideas, there are people selling refreshments in the park to those who can afford to buy the items being sold. I want you to experience this part of Kingston and tell me and Barracuda what you think about this market of ideas tonight."

At the Orange St. entrance to Parade, Harry could see many groups of people. Each group surrounded a preacher, but competing sounds from the groups reminded him of the Bible story of language confusion at the Tower of Babel. He sensed that what one group said had very little or no influence on another group. He eventually attended the meeting where Ras Joshua spoke. The recorded music to warm up that audience was different from anything he heard before. It had a strong beat, but a different rhythm from Kumina. The sound came from some big boxes electrified with loud speakers and referred to as sound system. The enthusiastic audience was not only prepared to listen, they were grooving to the beat. Ras Joshua spoke about long ago when all the people in the world were Black, before corruption and cold climate turned some people white. He spoke about heaven being an unreal idea made up by ministers who hide the truth under white collars they buttoned behind their necks rather than in the front. Those foolish ideas that made some Jamaicans sold everything they had to fly to heaven with the mad man called Bedward. After many of them crash landed, government put them away in mad house for the rest of their lives. But it was Joshua's following remarks that gained Harry's interest.

"Hear me now. Long ago Black man ruled Africa and build pyramids that white people from all over the world still find amazing. He had one underlying principle to his success. The stones at the bottom of the pyramid were like shoulders on which all the other stones stood. Those foundation stones were treated with dignity, some would say with more dignity than the pretty little white stones at the top. In Jamaican social pyramid, the decorative class of white people who sit on top of the burden bearing Black people, forget or ignore the reality that they cannot exist without us. Even worse, Black people forget that they are the foundation of this society and that every one of them is important to both God and man. We owe it to ourselves to protect and support the foundation of this modern pyramid. In the Bible, Cain who represented white people, murdered his brother Abel and told God he was not his brother's keeper. If it weren't so sad, one would think it funny that someone with a name like Abel couldn't defend himself against Cain. But I didn't write the Bible. Black people are not Cain, we are not white people, so everyone of us must be our brothers' keeper. If you agree with me, put up your hand in the air. Now turn to the man next to you and say, 'I am your keeper, brother.' One love! Rastafari!"

The man to whom Harry said he was his keeper, said his name was Mystic. While they embraced each other, another man took their picture with a camera that showed the image immediately. Harry's picture was visible, but there was no picture of Mystic even though the man snapped their picture twice. Mystic assured the photographer that nothing was wrong with the camera, but the mystical spirits of his African ancestors prevent his image from being captured. Another onlooker shouted, "He's an original. He can't be duplicated." That no-picture-photo experience was visible evidence to Harry that some Black people still had great power.

At the end of Ras Joshua's speech, so many people were jostling to get his attention that Harry waited a long time for his chance. He thanked Joshua for being his keeper and for reminding him of something else Tarta often said about white people. "They worked together like ants moving big pieces of food into their nest. When the job was too big for one ant, many ants combined their efforts to get the job done. Modern-day Black people don't follow that model. Each one tends to limit himself to what that individual can manage. When the problem was too big for one person to manage, he turned away in failure rather than succeeding with additional support. The smartest Black person can't win wars against a group of white people who unite their efforts to fight him. Black people need a new understanding of unity to break the mental chains that keep Black people in bondage." At the end of Harry's reflection on the speech, he concluded that Joshua and Tarta, his great-grandfather, had similar believes that unity among Black people could be an effective weapon against white people's oppression.

To clarify Harry's understanding of the sermon at Parade, Ras Joshua reflected on Harry's earlier experiences in the Market. "The first time I met you, the Cynic's idea of achieving liberty by being self-centered was dancing in your head. You just heard my ideas. It was not simply about unity. It emphasized the necessity of paying special attention to people at the bottom of society, because the height of social pyramids is directly related to the strength of the people at the bottom."

While trying to wrap his head around the idea that everyone at the bottom was important, Harry asked Joshua, "What could a selfish crook, a very poor person who barely had enough to eat, or a sick person contribute to a strong foundation?"

Joshua responded by comparing a weak person in society to a yam vine. "My parents specialized in growing Naga yam. They started by planting the yam head. When it sprouted above ground, it produced a vine that stretched along the ground in search of nutrients from sunlight to feed the yam growing underground. Yam vines on the ground were at risk of being destroyed as weeds, so experience taught my father to plant a pole near the yam head and train the vine to climb the pole. With that help, the yam vine got more sunlight and the yam grew much larger underground. Pumpkin received nourishment from a vine also, but dad allowed the pumpkin vine with large identifying leaves to creep along the ground, while the young pumpkins matured. He knew that pumpkin vines could not support the weight of mature pumpkins if they were suspended from a stick. The pumpkin vine would break prematurely, dad would lose his crop. He decided to leave the pumpkin vine on the ground and the yam vine on a stick. Similarly, it is necessary to cultivate people the way my father cultivated yams and pumpkins, by providing appropriate support."

Joshua also noted, "In Jamaica, and especially here in Kingston, we burry people like yam heads. Many who sprouted are chocked by weed like experiences rather than lifted to the sunshine. They yielded very little, leaving the need for a variety of solutions to problems associated with crooks, the poor, and the sick. No problem can be solved by ignoring it."

During their walk back to the hut at the rail yard Joshua explained, "Rastafarians are fighting for an outcome different from what most Jamaicans want. Rastas' primary goal is to find a better life in Africa, not in Jamaica. They resented the fact that white people stole them from Africa. They are determined to return to the motherland. They believed in cultivating people to flourish in Africa. That's why neither me nor Barracuda established a permanent residence in Kingston. We are in transition. We are not crazy. Our daily obligations are to find enough food, preferably at minimal cost, and to keep in touch with people who are interested in and paving the way for Black people to return to Africa. Until we return to Africa, we are not 'turn the other cheek' type of Jamaicans. We believe in fighting for justice by any means necessary. So, while we don't pick fights, we will defend ourselves to death. We will fight fire with fire."

Before they settled down for the night, the discussion focused on Harry's family background. Are his family members alive? Have they deserted him? Did he desert them? Both men heard him speak about Tarta. He described Tarta as his great-grandfather who told him many stories that were better than anything written in books. Tarta was a Maroon who believed that one day Black people would break the mental chains of slavery and be free. He told them he never met his father who ran away from plantation district out of fear that people would beat him to death for getting Harry's teenage mother pregnant. He told them about his mother's business activities that kept her so busy that she spent very little time attending to him. She hired many different people to watch over him, while she worked every day gathering products to sell in the market. One day, when he was much younger, she angrily asked God to put a curse on him, by turning him into a lazy, dirty, hairy animal that sleeps in trees. That curse followed him to Kingston where he ended up sleeping in a tree like the lazy animal called a sloth.

He reminded them that they were witnesses to that curse. They discovered him as a naked dirty boy living in a tree. Except for that one curse, his mother never did anything to hurt him. Her life was difficult, but she always found ways to overcome the challenges. The spirit of adventure stole her from him when she left Jamaica to find success in England. No one has heard from her since. In case they were wondering how this story relates to his living in Coronation Market, he gave them the answer. "My mother is a Maroon like me. Maroon spirits can communicate with one another, even though they are miles apart and even if they were dead. I'm convinced that my mother's spirit still lingered in the market and when her Maroon spirit finds my spirit, she will ask God to break the curse she put on me."

Ras Joshua brought a little more pragmatism to the conversation by asking the following question, "Did anyone go to the post office to check for mail? It could be that she wrote to Tarta or someone else in the district and was awaiting a response. She may have been trying to communicate by mail rather than through the Maroon spirit."

Harry was very surprised by that question, because no one in his family, except his mother, ever went to the post office five miles away for mail. He believed his mother knew that and would never write to them. She would also know there would be complications if family members told the post mistress they were expecting mail from someone in England with two different names—Matilda Mason or Virginia Johnson.

Barracuda shifted the inquiry to Harry's father. "Do you know your father's name?"

"His name is Victor Black," Harry told him.

Barracuda immediately turned to Joshua and said, "Take a good look at the boy and tell me who you see. Look on his forehead, his nose, mouth, and the shape of his face. You could put Victor's head on this boy's body and no one would know the difference." He continued to explain that he and Harry's father grew up together in Portland before they came to Kingston to find work.

"Victor Black was the youngest of Missah Amos and Miss Ruth six children. Him born in Manchioneal, a district inna di eastern parish of Portland. Rumor has it that him faada descended from Nanny, the madda of Maroon warriors, that killed British soldiers many years ago to free Maroon people in Portland from slavery. His parents made good use of water and wood, two of the most precious commodities in that area. Sea water and river water provided food and recreation, but sea sport was different from river sport, partly because di sea water had space to swim, while di river flowing off rocks created many waterfalls that people in di area called Reach Falls. Some people still believe that Reach Falls is prettier than Dunn's River Falls at Ocho Rios, in di western part of di island. Him faada usually catch nuff fish on weekends fi feed di family, but we never liked fishing, because it tek too long fi catch a fish. Wi prefer fi swim on Saturday mornings when most people still a sleep. Wi compete fi beat each other at riding di biggest waves them. When we left di beach, we would go to Reach Falls fi rinse off di sea water. Usually, we start by jumping off di lowest falls fi build wi courage to jump off di highest ones. Most times when we look back at di jagged rock face on the way down to di pool of water, we realized how narrowly we missed death. But that near-death experience leff we wid a bigga high dan smoking a spliff; because, mentally each of us combined di effects of di jumper and di watcher.

"But all was not fun and games fi Victor. Him faada worked hard fi support him family and demanded similar efforts from di children in cultivating di ten acres of land inherited from his grandparents. Di land was fertile, being blessed with plenty rain and sunshine. Wid those gifts from God, it was up to Mr. Amos fi multiply them like di good man inna di Bible who multiplied his talents. The family always had nuff, nuff food, like yams, sweet potatoes and bananas at Victor's house. But I enjoyed the special treats: guineps, jack fruits, jimbilin, june plums, mammee, mangoes, naseberry, otaheite apple, soursop, star apple, sweetsop, tamarind and water melon. After me and Victor ate di fruits, one of us would climb a coconut tree, pluck young sperm jelly coconuts from the tree and hold them while sliding down the tree. We gently placed them on the ground to preserve the potency of the water in them. We would then chop them open and quench our thirst with the cool jelly coconut water, before eating the soft jelly meat.

"In addition to cultivating di land, Missah Amos had another business of burning charcoal. That was di hardest work of all. Him produce an average of fifty bags of charcoal every two weeks fi sell people in Kingston who nuh have nuh wood fi cook dem food.

Di work included; cutting down huge trees, preferably, acacia and guango trees, chopping them into small blocks, digging a deep hole in di ground fi make a kiln, carrying di wood to the kiln, cutting grass to cover di wood, putting several layers of earth over di grass and allowing a little opening to light a fire in di kiln. When di fire cools after three days, di next job is to bag di coal and sell it to higglers who retail it in Kingston.

"Victor worked hard for his father every day before and after school, with my help. After a while we got tired and left the district for Kingston, where we expected life to be easier. We each had relatives in East Kingston and we lodged with them while we looked for work. In between looking for work, we attended various meetings about injustice to dark skin Jamaicans and how Christianity keeps us in slavery to the white man. Before long we accepted the idea that the first people on earth were Black and that we, not white people were God's chosen children. We became missionaries of the movement, determined to help others see di light. We regarded work as a secondary interest, so we eked out a living selling weed, playing dominoes some nights and betting on competing cyclists at Race Course on Friday nights. We enjoyed those Friday night races as the most fun of the week. Unlike the meetings at Parade, people came together for a good time, rather than to resist oppression. The fun increased when we bet on a rider who overcame various odds, came from behind in the last few seconds, and won. We were lucky to pick more winners than losers. On one of those happy Friday nights, a woman lured your dad to move to the parish of Saint Thomas. That was four years after we came to Kingston. The next thing I know, him follow di skirt to the district where you were born. I don't think that woman was your mother, because the name Virginia don't ring a bell in my memory. Secondly, she was not a teenager at di time.

"After Victor left, mi and Joshua continued promoting di Black man's back to Africa redemption. Then many years later, out of nowhere, Victor showed up wid di spirit of a beaten man. Him refused fi discuss what was wrong wid him, but he was obviously haunted by what him was running from. We knew he was not a violent man. We also thought he wouldn't be that upset if police caught him wid some weed. But now that I see you, Victor's depression makes sense. He violated his own rules by breeding a young girl and not staying around to shoulder his responsibilities to the baby mother and child, the way his father did. Even worse, your young mother was not yet a woman. He was ashamed. Next thing I knew, him stow away on a banana boat to Portsmouth, England."

Barracuda continued to explain that another reason why Victor went to England was to learn some white man's tricks to use in Africa. He was upset that white men in England who didn't grow bananas found ways to get the best bananas from Jamaica and leave residents with the rejects. That's a different kind of trickery than slavery. White men dug up the ground and discovered more than dirt. They found various kinds of rocks and minerals; gold, silver, petroleum, natural gas, and before you blink your eyes, they were using those material to enrich themselves and live more comfortably than most Black people. Black man knew how to make little wooden boats float a few miles from shore in calm waters when they went fishing. But white man got big, big ships even with heavy loads to float in the oceans from one continent to the next. He made heavy airplane fly in the sky. By contrast, Maroons were smart enough to send messages through conch shells from Portland to St. Thomas, but white men sent their signals from England to any part of the world. According to Victor's last letter to Barracuda, He learned some tricks about electricity while making radios and TVs in a factory.

What Harry heard about Victor Black filled him with mixed emotions. By going to England on his way to Africa, Victor put the greatest distance between himself and his responsibilities to Virginia and his son, even if he were the person anonymously sending envelops with money occasionally to Virginia. But Harry liked the fact that his dad seemed smart and funny. He also felt jealous that Barracuda knew more about his dad than he did. Before that story, Harry felt like an untethered kite drifting in the wind. But at that moment he felt a budding connection to a father, while adjusting to the lost connection with his mother.

Throughout Barracuda's story Ras Joshua listened with the prettiest smile Harry ever saw. Joshua evidently knew the story of Victor

Black. But there seemed to be a spring of joy bubbling up within him as he listened and looked at Harry. When he broke his silence, he said, "Harry, you are not a jacket." That was his way of saying Harry was not a bastard child, but the biological child of Victor Black. He thought Jah directed him and Barracuda to Harry's resting place in the tree, so that they could rescue the child of a brethren. His next project will be to have Harry's picture taken and sent as a surprise to Victor.

Their discussion did not purge Harry of his desire to return to the market and wait for a message from his mother. The men seemed to be aware of Harry's inclination and embarked on a strategy to engage him in activities outside the market. Their first order of business was to prepare Harry to have his picture taken and sent to his father. Instead of going to a barber for a haircut, they took Harry to someone who would preserve the length of his hair by matting and braiding it into dreadlocks. Harry had never thought of becoming a Rasta, so when his mind created a mental picture of dreadlocks on his head, he had difficulty recognizing himself. Then he was concerned about his appearance to others who knew him previously, and people he would be meeting for the first time. The uncertainty of how he would be received, and how he would react to the reception without a cultivated response, made him sad. But the emotional sadness developed into physical symptoms. He had an indescribable sensation in his head that he never felt before. Then the veins in his neck began pushing against the skin in opposition to potential dreadlocks hanging on his neck. He felt snakes crawling on the back of his neck and occasionally used his right hand to brush away imaginary crawling objects. He developed a noticeable twitch, as the utterances of his body became more audible than his words. His spasms caught the attention of Joshua and prompted him to ask, "Who is tickling your neck? I look every time you twitch, but I can't see the duppy."

Harry surrendered to his new hairstyle as silently as the proverbial lamb to the slaughter and the compliant sheep before its shearer in the Good Book of Isaiah.

During the restyling of his hair, Harry still felt the urge to re-establish a connection with his mother in the market. That created a conflict within him that he had difficulty reconciling. One part of him accepted the reality that his mother was not physically in the market nor in Jamaica, but the other part of him refused to accept the fact that she had gone. His experience reminded him of One Foot Tony whom the British recruited to fight in World War II. Tony returned to Jamaica with only one leg. The other one was blown off below the knee by enemy fire. But many days Tony complained about having pain in the missing leg. Everybody used to laugh at him for making up stories about this persistent pain in a non-existent body part. But recently, scientists say One Foot Tony told the truth. People can feel pain in a phantom limb.

Those reflections brought Harry back to reconciling his feelings about his mother's presence in the Market, even though he knew she was not physically there. During the years when his mother traveled to Kingston, he mentally retained her presence while she was physically absent. He conditioned his body to her absence by the work his mind did in preparing him for her return. He would anticipate interesting stories about new customers who chose her products rather than products of her competitors, stories about new experiences, insights into new adventures, and best of all, new treats. The mental joy preceded the physical joy of his mother's return. He did not feel hunger, he did not need to sleep, he was not tired of waiting. His mind kept reminding him of the past, but now his body refused to be deceived by feelings that are inconsistent with current reality. That condition left him drowning in a well of sadness that sapped his energy, leaving him as listless as a sloth.

After the braiding ordeal which lasted several hours, Joshua and Barracuda took Harry to a photographer on Orange Street for a picture-taking session. Harry never had his picture taken before, so he was uncomfortable posing for a picture. The mental conflict with his new hairstyle made his composure more difficult. Snapper, the photographer, sensing the discomfort, offered a solution. "I will shoot pictures of the older men first, then pictures with you and them, and finally, of you alone. The camera will love the sparkle in your eyes."

After Snapper took many pictures of Harry and the men together, he said, "I am going to show you a picture and ask you to think what you like about it." He showed Harry the picture of a pretty young woman who had just completed a successful dive at Dunn's River Falls. He allowed a few minutes for Harry to look at the picture before commenting, "This picture did not capture the young woman's mental courage to jump off the cliff and over the falls. It captured the joy of her success. The thing that captures my attention is not only the fact that her clothes are clinging tightly to her shapely body, dripping wet from head to toes. What leaps off the paper is the joy reflected in her eyes and her smile. Maybe that's why every time I look at her picture, the scowl on my face disappears and I have difficulty controlling my desire to say something nice to her, even though she can't hear me. You are seeing her picture for the first time; how do you feel about her daring dive? Do you share her joy? What do you feel like telling her to make her feel good about her accomplishment?"

Before Harry could answer, Joshua and Barracuda humorously cried, "That's not fair to us, brethren. You took our picture before giving us a chance to reflect on that beautiful woman!"

While Harry joined them in hearty laughter, the photographer snapped several pictures of Harry as the muscles in his face relaxed with more natural smiles.

Snapper joyfully exclaimed, "These pictures of you are among the best I have ever taken! You will love the Harry you see."

CHAPTER TWO

Back Home on the Plantations

The news of Harry's disappearance quickly spread from one end of Plantation Village to the other like wildfire in a sugarcane field. Sparks from hundreds of loose lips were flying everywhere and burning everyone's ears. Tarta was standing in the center of that flame when he failed to answer questions about his great-grandson, Harry, with nothing more than "him gone." He gave no hint of why, when, or where Harry was gone.

It's more than three weeks since Harry's playmates and neighbors saw him, but he popped into their minds multiple times each day. After each occurrence, people asked themselves and one another, "Why isn't Tarta looking for him? Why hasn't he asked for our help?"

They were increasingly impatient with his limited response. Some people, including Chatty-Chatty Catherine, said, "Tarta naa act right, because dis is not di first time people hear say one of him family member is gone. Mi still memba di news when people say him daughter, Elizabeth, gone. Den Mamma him beloved wife, gone. Next, Virginia, him only granddaughter, gone. Now, Harry, him great-grandson, gone. Di family first, second, third and fourth generations, gone. All a we still member say him never use nothing like silence nor dead people shroud, fi cover up the disappearance of him daughter Elizabeth and him beloved wife, who everybody call

Mamma. Instead, him invited all a wi in a di district fi come to dem public funerals and burials in him backyard. The difference between how Tarta use to act then and how him acting now, is like day and night. I will bet my last shilling that something is really wrong."

While neighbors speculated why Virginia and Harry were gone, and reasons why Tarta was silent about where they are, Tarta's mind had been searching tirelessly for answers to both his missing family members and the plight of his friends and neighbors whom he saw each day. From his gnomon-like fixed position on the plantation's economic sundial, he could more accurately tell what time it was financially than any other worker. He was troubled by his knowledge of friends and neighbors who were broke and living in less than hand-to-mouth conditions. He knew their experience. Working sunup to sundown daily, under backra men's watchful eyes contributed to their failing health. He knew they earned little more than pain and sorrow, while plantation owners reaped saddlebags of cash from their labor. He knew also that those prevailing conditions limited the Village's appeal to newcomers. But he was uncertain why very few residents, other than his family members, refused to leave the Village voluntarily or even prematurely by death. Ironically, even he was in the valley of decision, trying to decide whether to endure known hardships in Plantation Village, or to cut ties with the village and run. Given all that he endured, there was only one explanation why he hadn't left the district. The midwife who delivered him planted his navel string under a cotton tree down by the river.

According to Larry, "Tarta born and grow in Plantation Village, but him have a love-hate relationship with di place long before him family members gone. Him hate local barriers, both those people see and those dem imagine. Barriers dat limit di freedom him hear about in Kingston, only forty miles away. Truth be known, there was no visible obstacle like old slave chains or barbed wire fence holding him back. Him wasn't tied up like a fierce bull in cow pastures. But, something invisible in his head was holding him back. Him was also restrained by di lay out of di land and di way plantation owners controlled where him live and when him work. Their control left him totally dependent pon rich people who own plantations west, north and east of di village. Their actions not only controlled his life, but the life of everyone in the district.

"If you catch him at the right time, you could hear him talk about his life as a young man in di district, di many challenges him meet up face-to-face, especially when him tried to move from his parent's house to find his own place to live. Him didn't have no choice but a tiny plot of land, that big plantation owners hesitated to lease or to rent him. The agreement limited him to live in a confined area of the district, almost like a prisoner, on the worst lands, nearly surrounded by plantations on three sides. His source of money and his survival would always be tied to decisions that the land owners made.

"Him walk proud fi show off him broad shoulders on his five feet eleven inches body. People would have to be blind not to see many years of hard labor in his muscular arms. But him found it frustrating that the money him make from hard labor on the plantations did not enable him fi build the house him wanted. Undiscouraged, him decide to build his house by himself without advice form people with more experience. He built it little by little over a long period of time, shedding buckets of sweat each day. Him put a lot of thinking into the size of the house, what shape it should have and what material to build it with. But him decided in the end, to build the house him could afford. When him started the building, him cock sure him could do it alone. But after a while, reality catch up with him and force him to accept that some things him could not do by himself. But many times, unreliable help and the slow speed of the construction frustrated him."

Daniel remembered that Tarta started constructing the foundation without stabilizing sills and without help from anyone. "He reinforced the base with a mixture of clay, white marl, and loose dirt. He mixed the loose dirt with cow manure to keep it sticking together and limit the potential spread of unwanted dust when the mixture was dried. He built the house with a rectangular shape, typical of other houses in the district. But unlike some that were framed with logwood, cedar, or other hard wood; he substituted bamboo, a more accessible and lighter alternative to hard wood. By choosing bamboo, he avoided the daunting task of cutting down big trees and stripping them to get lumber to frame his house.

"His next concern was the roof. He observed that most houses in the district had hip shape, but few had triangular A-shape extending well below the roof line along the wider sides of those houses. It struck him that those houses with extended roofs needed less wood to build their sidings. So, he copied the cheaper style. He quickly sought and accepted help thatching his roof before completing the sidings, in hopes of preventing puddles of rainwater from ruining the foundation. He thatched the roof with guinea grass, in contrast to many that were thatched with coconut palm leaves and a few covered with zinc. After he completed the roof, he resumed work on the sidings and completed them with interlaced bamboo strips. He daubed the wattle with a mixture of white marl and clay to prevent wind and rain from seeping into the house."

Neighbors speculated that he built the house with two rooms, in preparation for a family. He built one room as a common area where family members could assemble when it was too dark or otherwise inconvenient to be in the yard. The other room could be the family's bedroom. The kitchen would be built later as a separate structure for both cooking and eating meals. But until then, cooking would be done under a shed, not far from the house that offered protection from rain. The improvised stove consisted of a fireplace with three large stones on which the three-legged pot sat over a stock of blazing firewood.

He did not build a bathroom. His family members would be expected to wash themselves behind the house in the evenings, when neighbors would have difficulty seeing them naked. Some yards had outdoor pit latrines. But until he built one, his family members would squat over chamber pots, and then dump the excrement in crab holes or in stagnant ponds in the backyard. Unfortunately, those ponds became breeding grounds for the anopheles mosquitoes that infected their victims with the malaria virus.

Tarta's initial small plot of land include his house, but no vegetable garden. He aspired to enlarging his plot with additional land when adjoining neighbors died. He, like most residents in the district, became a subsistence farmer, renting additional plot of land in another location to cultivate seasonal crops for food and year-round cash crops. Seasonal food crops included tubers—yams, sweet potatoes, and cassava. They also included fruits—typically, mangoes, breadfruit, soursop, and naseberry. The year-round cash crops were bananas and plantains.

People in the district could see that Tarta worked constantly at various jobs on the plantations to earn necessary funds to pay his debts to the owners for the two parcels of land he rented. Unlike Tarta, some residents stubbornly resisted the economic need to work on the plantations. They chose instead to be full-time subsistence farmers on parcels of land rented from the plantation owners. But they did not fare much better than Tarta, because they competed unfavorably against plantation owners who flooded the market with similar products grown under more favorable conditions. First coconut trees already growing on the rented and leased plots, owned by plantation owners, overshadowed fruit trees and tuberous plants grown by both Tarta and full-time subsistence farmers. Second, coconut trees had a cluster of several thousand adventitious roots sucking moisture from the surrounding soil. They starved plants cultivated by tenant farmers of necessary moisture. Third, plantation employees carelessly trampled food crops cultivated by the tenant farmers when reaping coconuts on tenanted plots. Such exploitation reduced the earnings of tenant farmers, leaving them with barely enough for hand-to-mouth living.

Often, owner representatives penalized Tarta and other tenant farmers for unauthorized use of a few coconuts that fell unto the rented plots. But they did not compensate tenant farmers for involuntarily clearing weeds from around coconut trees overhanging the cultivated plots. Those penalties ignored tenant farmers important contributions to the plantations. Their unfair treatment added to innumerable other injustices.

Neighbors also observed that Tarta and many other tenant farmers waited in long lines early Monday mornings to compete for various jobs as day laborers on the plantations. When hired, some dug trenches to enable rain water to irrigate the banana fields. Those less literate memorized the dimensions of the trenches and how many they dug. They often relied on their more literate children or grand-children to calculate the measurements and estimate the accuracy of wages they received.

Some picked coconuts off trees with hooks at the end of very long sticks or by hand after climbing the tallest trees. They husked coconuts with gardening implements such as hoes, machetes, axes, or other improvised equipment to remove the brown fibrous covering that encases the inner shell. They worked in the factory to extract coir from the fibrous coconut husk, used to make floor mats, brushes, and mattress stuffing. They extracted oil from dried coconut meat, called copra, and made coal from the burned coconut shell.

Some worked in sugarcane fields, digging six-inch furrows to plant sugarcane buds at intervals of approximately one yard. For the next two years before harvesting, they systematically cleared weeds that could stifle the growing sugarcane plants. During the harvesting of the crop, between December and May, they bent low, several hours each day in the scorching sun, to cut the mature stalk as close to the ground as possible. They loaded sugarcane stalks on trucks to the destination factory where the owners make molasses and Jamaican rum.

Some cleared weeds from banana fields and monitored the development of banana trees from suckers to maturity. They watched soft trunks mocking hard wood trees as they grew sturdier each day. Then spiral leaves unfurled from the stems, followed several months later by blossoms which turned into fingers. Fingers then turned into hands too heavy to be supported in an upright position by the stem. When the weight of the bunches turned them upside-down, laborers provided necessary support to prevent the weight of the fruit from uprooting the trees. They monitored the size and color patterns on the banana fingers, which became bulkier before the color gradually changed from light green to yellow as they ripened. During the mat-uration of the fruits on the trees, Tarta and other laborers determined the ideal time for reaping the bananas for shipment overseas.

Because the people seeking work outnumbered the available jobs, plantation owners had the financial advantage of choosing the workers they wanted, deciding how many days they would be employed and how much to pay them. Those chosen worked eight-hour days. Their pay averaged one shilling per day. At the end of each day, they experienced their exploitation by plantation owners as sadistic rape in a primitive society.

Many who were unemployed, entertained themselves under shade trees, away from their yards. One location was near the local grocery store, nicknamed Bulla Shop. It was the district's center of social activities. It adjoined the main road on a flat piece of land that was in stark contrast to the hills and gullies in other areas of the inhabited district. It was the pickup and drop-off location for people traveling to and from the district on public transportation. Adults addressed the owner of the shop as Bulla Watson, but children in deference to his age called him Missa Bulla.

Friday afternoons were usually busy in the shop. The delivery van with freshly baked bulla arrived just when children were returning from school with lunch money saved to buy fresh bulla. There was a stampede to the shop counter. There was no queue. Everyone approached the counter, determined to be served first. There were raucous shouts.

"Give me one bulla!" one said.

"Me want two bullas," said another.

"Me was here first!" other voices shouted.

"Take it easy, don't worry. You will get all the bulla you need when it's your turn," Bulla Watson said.

Suddenly, Papa John and Mamma Son started to fight. "You knock mi bulla out a mi han," Papa John said as he punched Mamma Son in the face.

Mamma Son dropped his books, picked up the bulla off the ground and stuffed it in Papa John's mouth while shouting, "Here is you dutty bulla. Nyam it wid the dirt!"

Bulla Watson intervened to end the fight. He reassured them, "I have enough bulla for everybody!"

Although the shop was nicknamed Bulla Shop, it sold a variety of other grocery items, including salted meats, pigs' tails, pigs' feet, cow tripe, salted dried cod fish, herrings, mackerels, flour, sugar candy, and rum. People ate bulla as a favorite snack for three reasons. First, their stomachs felt full quickly, especially when they ate it with ripe banana, avocado, or a piece of dried coconut. Second, long after they swallowed the bulla, the ingredients—white flour, brown sugar, ginger, butter, and vanilla—lingered on their tongues in playful hide-go-seek. They also loved bulla because it was cheap, costing only half a penny.

Given the fact that houses in the district did not have facility to store perishable groceries, people made frequent visits to Bulla Shop to purchase or credit items for the day's meal. The visits also provided opportunities for shoppers to socialize with friends and catch up on the latest gossip.

At a table under a shade tree beside the shop, Duppy-man played dominoes with Henry. He suddenly shouted, "I blocked the game! Henry dem pieces ina you han dead now. What's your count? Mi have double blank and one ace. If you can't beat that, sound the alarm. Mi beat you six love."

A dozen people watching the game laughed as Henry responded to Duppyman, "Mi draw a bad han and you kill di double six and di double five whey mi have. You lucky dis time and I will buy you a shot of rum. But don't mek this win get to you head. Member say mi beat you every game last week."

A short distance from the domino table, a few teenage boys tested their homemade roller skates on the paved main road. Others flew homemade kites, with tails betraying pieces of their mothers' old curtains or bed sheets.

Unexpectedly, Bulla Watson shouted this announcement from inside the shop, "Listen everybody! A banana boat drop anchor at Bowden wharf tomorrow and will hire two dozen stevedores to load the boat with bananas. Come, gi mi yuh names pon dis piece of paper if yuh waah fi work. I will send Ricky Jones with it to the harbor master first thing in the morning."

Soon after Bulla Watson made the announcement in the shop, word spread to the men playing dominoes. Game stop brop, instantly! Men jumped up from the domino game, dashed into the shop shouting their names. "Randy Janes! Manny Hail! Steven Will!"

In addition to the Bulla shop location, people hung out in two other recreation spots, the cow pasture and the beach. Young boys and girls hung out at the far side of the district, in a cow pasture. There, they played separate games. Boys played cricket, soccer, foot racing, and a running game called Chevy Chase. That game required a team of four or more boys on opposing sides taking turn to capture the opponents' base before being tagged. The best players could run very fast and avoid being tagged by dodging efforts of one or more adversaries who tried to tag them. They played with a watchful eye on potentially unfriendly bulls that roamed the pasture near the playing field, especially when heifers and cows were in heat. Girls played handball, jump rope, hide-and-seek, hopscotch, and running games. Their disputes, unlike the boys, did not end in physical fights, but a war of words such as "cut eye cut eye cyaan cut me in two, penny, penny cyaan buy mi shoes." They generally used the phrase in response to insulting gestures like looking at the offended person from the corners of one's eyes, then turning away in disgust.

People of all ages hung out at the most popular recreation spot, the beach. Unlike experiences in the village surrounding Bulla shop, or the cow pasture, the beach provided both recreational opportunities and part-time work. People engaged in activities of choice rather than obligation. It was a place to drown sorrows and wash away pain.

No one loved the beach more than Harry's mother, Virginia, when she was fifteen years old and no one loved her more than Tarta and Mammy Lou, her grandparents. Each one often said, "She is the apple of my eyes." But there were two significant omens associated with her birth. First, on October 29, 1929, the day before she was born, things turned topsy-turvy. Money systems in the United States collapsed and started something called the Great Depression. It affected people all over the world, including Jamaica, where it combined with the oppressive plantation system to stifle people's development. Second, during childbirth, her mother, Elizabeth, died unexpectedly. In those days, pregnant women did not receive expert prenatal care, and the skills of untrained midwives were limited to hearsay from older folks. According to local rumors, the delivery began with the baby nurse saying, "Elizabeth, from the looks of things down there, you are ready to give birth to this baby. How do you feel?"

Elizabeth's only response was an agonizing groan, "O-o-o-h!"

The baby nurse commented, "She is groaning! She is having labor pains. Mammy, boil some water in a pot as quick as you can. We need it to wash away the germs before welcoming the baby germ-free into the world. Oh yes! I can see the baby's head. The water cool yet? Elizabeth is frothing at the mouth and her contractions are not strong enough to push out the baby. I will have to help her by pulling the baby out."

"Mind you break the pickney neck," said Mammy.

The baby nurse continued, "Elizabeth, keep pushing harder. I'm trying to get a good grasp of the head. I'm here to help you. Push!"

Six hours later, the midwife was still shouting, "Push!" As she extracted Virginia without realizing that the baby's mother had already died. No autopsy was done to determine the cause of death. No one knew what had happened inside Elizabeth's body to cause so much bleeding, which may have resulted in her death.

Virginia's grandparents raised her. She lived a happy life with family and friends, an experience complemented by Sunday school and elementary school activities. Although she reached the highest class in elementary school with a good record, no one offered her additional educational or work-related opportunities. Unlike other parishes in the island, St. Thomas had neither government sponsored nor private high school. It was not in the interest of the plantation owners, one of whom was the Custos, the highest-ranking civil officer in the parish. So, although the knowledge Virginia acquired in elementary school exceeded the requirements of a plantation worker, she had limited choices for gainful employment anywhere but on the plantation. Alternatively, she could be a live-in companion with a man who eked out a living on the plantations. But because her grandparents did not require her to do field work or to cook, her field and domestic abilities were not highly developed. She would not be the ideal asset on the plantation nor the typical live-in companion.

Fortunately for her, she still had time to have fun with her friends before grappling with grown-up decisions, but she had to request her grandparent's permission and tell them where she was going and with whom.

"Mammy, I'm going to the beach for a swim with Lucy." Virginia informed her grandmother Saturday morning.

"Okay, but don't go to Cutter Point. The sea is very rough there and it's rocky. Also, dangerous sharks and barracudas like to hang out there. Babbo lost his leg out there, and if it were not for God's grace, he could have lost his life."

"We will be careful!" she replied. She took a change of clothes with her as she left to meet Lucy.

Saturday morning at the beach was usually pulsing with activities, both seen and unseen. The competing sensory activities demand attention and most often, responses from eyes, ears, noses, and sometimes the entire body. Some people's eyes looked on the frilly waves rushing to the shore. Some people's ears welcomed the resounding crashes of the water on the beach and the chorus of joyful response as water rushed over people's feet or their entire bodies. Some people took deep breaths of the sea air with its peculiar mixture of salts, discarded shells of animals, logs, and fish tackles that have been washed ashore. But the background sulfuric smell of the surrounding mangroves and their reflection in the water hovered over all those sensations. Those trees, well suited for growing near the shoreline, thrived on saltwater. To get as much saltwater as possible, they grew aerial roots that stretched from their branches to the seabed. With two sets of roots, those trees resisted tropical force winds and formed a buffer for communities near the beach and a habitat for birds. Their reflection in the surrounding blue Caribbean water, backlighted by Jamaican sunrise and sunset, remained an unforgettably definition of natural beautiful.

People on the shore saw non-swimmers near the water's edge digging for cockles to make soup later in the day. Some making sand castles, while others waded timidly in the water as the ebbing tide washed the sand over their feet. Teenage boys rode the waves or splashed one another's faces with relentless somersaults they called Pupa Lick. Fishermen on the shore plaited bamboo strips into fish pots to be left at sea for two or three days, before harvesting the fish caught in the pots. Some fishermen waded a short distance from the shore before casting their fishing nets to catch fish. Some repaired their nets on the shore, while others could be seen hauling nets from their boats to the shore with the catch of the day. Still, others returned to shore after a night at sea, with fish caught the old fashion way—with hooks and lines.

It was not uncommon to hear a fisherman yelling, "Turtle prime! Turtle prime! Mi catch a good size male turtle. Come swallow down him prime with some white rum fi strengthen your manhood."

As the announcement got the attention of young and older men, many of them rushed to get a portion of the turtle's slippery genitals and swallow it uncooked with a swig of over-proof white rum. Local men relished the love potion in anticipation of the right moment. With that ritual, those men signaled to women and competing men that their sexual abilities were fortified with the sexual prowess and endurance of a methodically slow turtle.

Usually the catch of the day yielded more fish than district residents could purchase with wages earned on the plantation. For that reason, some fishermen traveled to neighboring districts to sell the excess fish.

After swimming for half an hour with Lucy, Virginia noticed a quieter group of people further along the beach.

"Lucy, let's have a race to where those quiet people in white are gathered," Virginia said.

"I can't swim that far, but I will compete against you by running on the sand," Lucy replied.

"That wouldn't be fair unless you give me a head start. Count to fifty before you start running," said Virginia.

"Okay!" said Lucy.

With that agreement, Virginia started to swim parallel to the shore on her way to the quiet gathering of people.

"Virginia! Virginia!" Lucy shouted. "I see Elder Adams and some people who worship at the Baptist Class House on Sundays. I wonder why some of them have on white clothes at the beach on a Saturday morning?"

"I can't hear you!" Virginia shouted, as a wave slapped her face.

"Look ahead! Elder Adams is having a church meeting at the beach!" Lucy shouted.

Although Virginia couldn't hear what Lucy said, she could see that Lucy was winning the race. She took a deep breath and dived out of sight to make it difficult for Lucy to determine her location. She surfaced soon after and shouted, "I will run with you."

While both ran toward Elder Adams and the people gathered with him, Lucy said, "I wonder why that branch sticking out of the water is not washed ashore like other debris in the sea. It just keeps on drifting parallel to the shore."

When Virginia looked at what Lucy described as a branch, she, too, was surprised, but quickly realized that the thing sticking out of the water was no branch, and it was getting closer to Elder Adams and the people surrounding him.

"It's a s-h-a-r-k!" Virginia yelled.

But as fate would have it, the baptismal ritual had begun, and Sister Mary was in the process of being immersed in the water by Elder Adams, who just heard the hysterical cry, "S-h-a-r-k!"

Seized with panic, Elder Adams lost the strength to raise Sister Mary's head above the water after the emersion. Additionally, he lost his balance when Sister Mary slipped from his grasp and when he accidentally stumbled onto an uneven surface of the seabed that led to a sinkhole. With both Sister Mary and Elder Adams thrashing about in the water, fear struck the assembled spectators. They were unprepared for the impending tragedy.

Brother Amos shouted a prayer, "Masa God, please save your children gathered here in obedience to your call. You saved Jonah in the belly of that big ole whale for three days, so you know how fi save people from the watery grave!"

Then Sister Angela shouted a refrain, "Yes, Lord, we know this job is bigger than the one in Nineveh, because you have fi save two people now from a shark, not one degge person inna di belly of a whale!"

Suddenly, without warning and at great risk to herself, Virginia dove into the water. She grabbed Sister Mary's skirt, but the skirt gave way. She reached for Sister Mary's flailing legs, but failed to grasp her, because Sister Mary was kicking so furiously. She eventually grabbed Sister Mary's head and dragged her to a shallow area where Sister Mary could stand with her head above the water. Immediately after rescuing Sister Mary, she returned and rescued Elder Adams just before he stumbled into the sink hole.

Still traumatized by the near-death experience, Elder Adams turned to the baptismal candidates and spectators and said in a feeble voice, "God moves in mysterious ways, His wonders to perform. Every one of you witnessed how Satan tried to interfere with the work of God. But you will now be able to testify that God is victorious every time. When we gather in worship tomorrow we will seek God's guidance on the next date for the baptism that Satan interrupted today. Virginia, you were God's angel of mercy today. We thank you from the bottom of our hearts for allowing God to use you successfully like He used Miriam to protect baby Moses from death by Pharaoh. Amen! Amen! I'm sure I will not be the only one telling Mammy and Tarta about your part in today's salvation story."

News of Virginia's heroics at the beach quickly spread through the district. When she returned home, Mammy and Tarta had already heard that she rescued Elder Adams and Sister Mary from both the shark and the watery grave. In gratitude for God's blessings on their granddaughter, Mammy and Tarta planned a Kumina celebration of the event with neighbors and friends.

CHAPTER 3

Ominous Storm

Virginia did not work in the fields. She worked in and around the yard, before and after school. Her morning activities included fetching water from a nearby spring early in the morning to fill a container in the kitchen; cleaning the chicken coop; and feeding a dozen hens, two roosters, and numerous chickens with dried corn, grated dry coconuts, and water. Her grandparents assigned her those chores for two basic reasons. First, to discourage any latent interest Virginia may have in working on the plantations. The other more positive reason was to nurture alternative skills that would make Virginia self-reliant. For her final assignment each evening, except Saturday and Sunday, she lit firewood under a pot of water, that would be hot enough to cook the evening meal immediately after Mammy and Tarta came home from the field.

One fateful evening, after the miraculous beach event and before the planned celebration, Virginia could not find the match to light the firewood. Unrelenting in her efforts, she went to her neighbor as she has done many times before, for a stick of match to light the firewood. This time was different. A frightening thunderstorm erupted without warning as she got near to Mas Victor's house.

Usually, before a storm in Plantation district, dark clouds appeared in the east and spread quickly to blacken the entire sky.

Nightingales, barble-doves, ants-quits, hawks, and other birds would be singing their bird songs to the rapid syncopation of woodpeckers drumming on tree trunks with their bills. Crickets and frogs would join the chorus at unpredictable intervals, as the unrehearsed choir made spontaneous sounds of various half notes along the chromatic scale. Then as wind shook the trees, rustling leaves added background to the cacophony of sounds. Leaves on coconut trees whistled at a higher pitch than the broader leaves on breadfruit trees. Banana leaves added lower notes as they flopped like giant wings in vain efforts to gain thrust for lift off. Finally, there would be the crescendo of thunder and heavy downpour of rain.

The prelude never occurred. In the short time it took fifteen-year-old Virginia to walk from where she felt the first raindrops to Mas Victor's house, she was soaking wet from unrelenting heavy showers of rain.

She banged the door of Mas Victor's house and shouted, "Please let me in!"

He quickly opened the door to rescue her. "Come in out of the rain, daughter, and take off the wet clothes in the next room before you catch a cold. Here is the shirt off mi back. It's big enough for you to wrap yourself in while your clothes a dry."

He allowed her privacy to undress in a bedroom behind the entrance room. She undressed, wrung the water from her wet clothes, before hanging them on protruding nails in bamboo frame of the house. She prayed an unrealistic silent prayer that her clothes would be dry when the storm ended and certainly before Mammy and Tarta returned from the field. But she slowly adjusted to the reality that her clothes would not be dry when she left Mas Victor's house. She shuddered at the thought of putting on her wet dress and underwear. But she was determined not to put on her wet panty because of an old folk tale that women who wore wet panties could catch a bad cold in their bellies and die.

Virginia lost track of time. It seemed like forever since she had been partly naked and shivering in a corner of the back room, farthest from the opening to the front room. She felt drowsy and would be lulled to sleep by the syncopating beat of rain drops on the zinc roof, but for the cool winds blowing through the bamboo wattle frame of the house kept her shivering and awake. While she tried to sooth the itchy goose bumps all over her body, she heard Mas Victor asking from the front room, "You want some lemonade?" She felt grateful for the offer of lemonade from Mas Victor, but she hesitated to accept it because she felt embarrassed to be almost nude in his presence.

"Make it stay deh till mi clothes dry," she replied.

"Aren't you wearing the shirt I offered you?" he inquired.

"Yes, sah, but my underwear them still wet."

Surprised to hear that she would not accept the lemonade while she was partially undressed, he offered her the drink through the half-closed door. He also gave her a bit of adult advice, "Pickeny, di room no have no heat other than yu body. Teck yu clothes offa di nail dem behind di door, put dem on and lively up you self to the rhythm of the bandu drum, playing in the background by brada Shut. Your movements will make you clothes dem dry quicker."

She pondered his instruction briefly and partially accepted it as adult advice. She reached for her wet dress and slowly slipped it over her head, but its wetness felt uncomfortable. She took off the dress and replaced it on the nail.

She drank the pint-size can of lemonade quickly without savoring its taste. She placed the empty can on the ground beside her and cuddled up to make herself comfortable in a corner of the room. Suddenly, explosive thunder claps shook the entire house. Even worse, the accompanying lightning threatened to set the house on fire. She bolted from the room in a panic and sought refuge in Mas Victor's arms. As she clung to him, she began to feel a strange sensation. The ground under her feet was moving. Even the bamboo walls were spinning slowly around her. While she wondered if earthquake accompanied the storm, she began to feel tired.

"Yu body soon feel warm now, because mi put a likkle white rum inna di lemonade fi warm you up," Mas Victor assured her. "Can you hear di Kumina drum over di nex yaad? Budum budum, budum budum, budum budum. That sound like Breda Shut a play di baandu drum fi keep dupy ghosts outa di house when there is a storm." Virginia did not reply.

As they clung to each other against a table, their upper bodies shared one shirt. She wore the inside of the shirt he offered her earlier. He wore the outside of it against his chest. She comforted herself by clinging to him more tightly, after each flash of lightening and frightening peal of thunder. In that darkness that enveloped them, he became her only source of light and she responded with phototaxis attraction, like a firefly to a light bulb. She lingered in his invisible light.

She felt his shirtless chest against her. She felt the quickening pace of his heartbeat and playfully wondered how she could get her heart to beat in rhythm with his. She even surmised that wearing the shirt separated them far enough to impede the synchronization of their heart beats.

But while Mas Victor was bravely comforting her, she was unaware that he was also afraid. He feared the external threats of lightning and thunder. But he had a greater concern about his increasing urge to respond to Virginia's perceived need for intimacy. He did his best to deflect those thoughts. He felt the hardened nipples of her breast against his naked chest as she clung to him, but he excused it as her fearful response to the storm. He felt her warm breath on his earlobes and excused it as accidental, even though it reminded him of past romances. His beard mediated the feelings of her smooth cheeks against his, but he satisfied himself with the pleasure of its non-accidental gentleness. He thought her eyes would be most indicative of her sensual needs, but darkness hid the expression in her eyes as she comforted herself by playing with his beard.

With Virginia still clinging tightly to him, Mas Victor changed his standing position to sitting on the straw mat covering the ground floor. He stumbled and fell with his back on the mat, thus cushioning her fall. Virginia fell on top of him and remained motionless. She had never been that close to a man before. She worried that her weight was oppressive. Unexpectedly, for the first time she felt unusual stirrings in various parts of her body, although uncertain what to do about them. She had never even seen another couple that close. Although she shared a bedroom with Mammy and Tarta, she had never seen them embrace. She wondered when and where they were ever that close to each other as she was to Mas Victor. She and her friend Lucy were accustomed to making fun of the idea that boys and girls got close and did it in the bushes where no one could see them. But they never associated emotions with thoughts of doing it, so she remained clueless about what happened in those bushes.

When her thoughts returned to Mas Victor, Virginia could not summon the will to loosen her hold on him. She eventually realized that he did not seem to be uncomfortable with her lying on top of him, because he held her close to him with arms that felt strong enough to bind chords of wood. He even began to sing an old digging song in a trance-like lullaby in his continuing effort to comfort her.

"Sammy plant piece a corn down a gully,
Huh! Huh!
And it bere till it kill poor Sammy,
Huh! Huh!
Sammy dead! Sammy dead! Sammy dead, Oh!"

His lullaby song and his gentle massages reduced her physical and emotional tensions. In her more relaxed mode she reflected on Mas Victor's attentiveness and even imagined similarity to a protective mother hen gathering her chickens under her wings during rainstorms or whenever they were in danger. She even found comfort in the thought that Mas Victor was more like a hen than an indifferent rooster that never displayed any interest in protecting little chickens from danger.

The intensity of the storm seemed to be decreasing. But they felt certain it would return, even though they could not say how soon and with what strength. While their expectation of episodic storms lingered, both continued their quest for security in each other's arms. But soon after they felt a little more secure, they automatically became more conscious of their naked proximity to each other. Her body began asking questions that her mind could not put into words. But his body responded automatically with Morse code-like signals, that her body instinctively interpreted without the benefit of light or sound. Their rapid, but unanswered, questions continued for a while, because there were more questions than satisfying answers.

Their telepathic exchanges ended with the arrival of the tempting serpent. They, like Adam and Eve, succumbed to his temptation with that forbidden fruit. But howling winds in the background may have deafened their ears to any mysterious voice asking, "Where art though?" They only heard their own voices in alternating choruses. She was shouting, "Mas Victor! Mas Victor!" He responded with his kind of Hallelujah chorus, "Yes! Yes! Ye-e-e-s!"

With those joyful exclamations, Virginia was initiated into womanhood with Mas Victor's name written in bold letters in her memory. She felt the brail-like letters of his name when she dressed in her damp clothes, including her undergarments. She could not get him out her mind when she hurried home during the drizzling rain nor during the months that followed. Nothing else had ever been secretly locked in her consciousness before as the experience with Mas Victor. Their experience had become bigger than any secret she managed previously. In the past, she could manage little secrets like skipping school for the beach with friends, eating a meal at a forbidden neighbor's house, or visiting a neighboring district with friends without her grandparents' permission.

While reflecting on her stormy experience, she bathed herself behind the house with the rainwater collected in a wash pan. She had just completed her bath when her grandparents returned from the field. Tarta, her grandfather, went near to the kitchen and threw down a bundle of firewood he'd carried on his head from the field. Mammy, her grandmother, put down her load more quietly in the kitchen, because she carried the food harvested from the field.

"Virginia! Virginia!" Mammy called out, "where are you? Were you too scared to start the fire during the rainstorm?"

Her grandmother's question about starting the fire reminded her why she went to Mas Victor's house and why she forgot to ask him for matches. She responded, "I was very scared during the storm, but that's not why I didn't start the fire. I could not find the matches."

Mammy replied, "Oh! You couldn't find the matches because mi hide it fi save back few sticks inna de box. I didn't want to stop you from lighting the fire, but I did want Tarta to stop using the last few sticks of matches to light his pipe when he needed a smoke.

I'll get another box of matches after I take off these wet clothes." Mammy continued, "From me born me never see so much rainfall in one day. This rainfall could wash away all the sins in the district. It is Masa God's way cleansing the place and giving us a new start."

While Virginia was in the house putting on dry clothing, Tarta stocked the wood in the kitchen before he changed out of his wet clothes. It took Mammy a little while to get the fire started, because the firewood was wet. But she kept blowing on the sparks of fire until the wood began to flame. In between blowing on the fire, she asked Virginia, "What did you do during the storm?"

Virginia replied, "Me hide under the bed and worry if you and Tarta was safe."

Mammy explained her experience. "First thing me and Tarta did when the rain cloud burst was to make sure we weren't under a coconut tree, because we didn't want lightning fi strike us. Good thing Tarta recently thatched the roof of the hut with guinea grass, so we ran to the hut for shelter. The roof didn't leak, but some of the bamboo wattles on the side of the hut were missing, so we got wet when the wind blew in the rainwater. We got wetter on our way home because we left in the rain and it keep on falling on us all the way home. It never stopped falling."

After the fire started, Mammy put a large pot with water on the fire to cook green banana, yellow yam, and corn meal dumplings mixed with white flour. She also cooked ackee and salt fish in a smaller pot. By the time dinner was ready, everyone was very hungry. She served Tarta first. She filled his calabash dish full of boiled bananas, tightly needed cornmeal dumplings, and a generous amount of ackee and salt fish, richly spiced with home-grown scallions and very spicy bird peppers.

Before Tarta began to eat he called out to Mammy, "Give me a cup of hot pot water to break the gas in mi stomach." As soon as he drank the broth, he belched loudly, tapped his belly with his right hand to force himself to expel any remaining gas in his gut before he began to eat. Mammy served Virginia next. After she served herself, she and Virginia joined Tarta on the bamboo bench in the kitchen to eat their dinner. At the end of the meal, Virginia's task of cleaning up the dishes and tidy up the kitchen followed. But before she undertook that task, Mammy said to her, "Virginia, put some of the leftover food in a small calabash and take it to Mas Victor. I don't see any smoke coming from his kitchen, and I can't imagine him cooking this late."

"Yes, Mammy!" was Virginia's frightened response. Her whole body began to tremble with ambivalent feelings of fear and excitement as she grappled with the thought of revisiting Mas Victor. Should she knock on the door and leave the food at his door before Mas Victor opened the door? Should she pretend that she took the food to his house, but he did not open the door, so she brought the food back? As she grappled with Mammy's instruction and the alternatives she contemplated, obedience to Mammy trumped her ambivalence. She left the food at Mas Victor's doorway without notifying him that she'd brought it.

She resisted the impulse to talk to anyone about her stormy night with Mas Victor. She was torn between gratitude for his loving protection during the storm and embarrassment that he knew her more intimately than anyone else. While those emotions hung in the balance, she worried that he could deliberately or inadvertently share their experience as his conquest, during rum talk with other men at Bulla Shop. She also worried that those men would spread the news in the community. Will they drag her name in the mud? Will they share the gossip with her grandparents? What will her grandparents say and do when they hear? In addition to those worries, she was concerned about how to relate to Mas Victor in the presence of her grandparents without signaling to them that something had changed between her and that family friend. Each night, however, she lulled herself to sleep with the memory of him comforting her.

CHAPTER 4

Prelude to New Development

On the day Virginia celebrated her heroics at the beach, Mammy and Tarta planned a big feast and entertaining music. They butchered a young ram goat. Made soup with the goat head and the goat feet, and made a big pot of curry goat stew with the other parts of the goat. In addition to the curry, they seasoned the stew with a home-grown seasoning including spicy red and green peppers, thyme, scallion, tomatoes, and okra. Tarta roasted twelve macka breadfruits, pealed them and turned them into fufu by pounding them in a wooden mortar with a pestle. The finished product had a consistency of mashed potatoes or turn cornmeal. A man nicknamed Shut, because he seldom wore a shirt, and Daniel, brought their drums to the party. Daniel brought a bandu drum and Shut brought a playing cyas drum. Both drums had cylindrical shapes. They were made of very fine seasoned wood with one end tightly covered with well-preserved goat skins. Each player sat on his drums and beat the skins with his hands. The playing cyas skin was wrapped more tightly than the bandu drum, had a higher pitch and a variety of sounds depending on whether the drummer beat the edges or the middle of the drum. Typically, the drummer on the playing cast tended to be more of a showman; in the way he beat the drum to alter the sounds and modify the tempo of the dance. The Bandu drum player provided the rhythmic background to the playing cyas with two basic sounds. One sound was slightly higher than the other when the player pressed his heel against the skin on the drum to alter the sound.

Some people brought young jelly coconuts with lots of juice to cool the thirst of those too young to drink white rum. Others brought white rum to liven up people's palates and the party, but all were prepared to drink Mammy's homemade lemonade in which the brown sugar, honey, and lemons leave the taste buds begging for more.

"Shut, come make we warm up the drum dem while di food a cook!" Daniel shouted.

"Give me a minute fi drag a likkle more weed from the Chilung pipe," Shut responded.

Shortly after that exchange, both men faced each other on their drums and began their steady beat. They became the center of attention and people began gathering around them.

"Go, granny!" someone shouted as granny Mary started to shuffle her bare feet on the ground in a circle around the men beating the drums. The circle got wider as more people joined it. With the increased number of people in the circle, there was a noticeable change in Shut's face as he beat the playing cyas with more energy.

With his head bobbing from side to side, Shut began to sing, "Namuna, co que onto Tata, Namuna." He completed the chorus with the highest sound on the drum sounding "pom-pom, polomm-pom."

In response, the circle of dancers echoed Shut's words, "Namuna, co que onto Tata, Namuna pom-pom, polomm-pom."

Mammy signaled that the meal was ready by calling Virginia and Lucy to help her serve the food. "Bring me some calabash bowls, big enough to hold the fufu and the stew." The girls fetched the bowls and while everyone's attention was focused on the food, Mammy said, "The first serving goes to the ancestors buried in the back of the yard. Take one calabash of food and a glass of white rum and leave it on mi mother's grave to mek her know say we welcome her at this special celebration."

After that ritual, Mammy dished out the goat head soup first. Some men believed the soup was an aphrodisiac and was careful not to spill a drop of it on the ground. The second course was the mixture of fufu and curry goat stew. The girls dutifully served the men first and then the women. Everyone used their fingers as utensils to put the stew into their mouths. It was obvious that people without teeth had no need to chew their food very long, because the okra made the sauce slippery and the food easy to swallow.

Virginia was careful not to serve Mas Victor, but he called her, "Virginia, ask Mammi to give me likkle more of the goat head soup and bring it come fi me."

"Yes, sir," Virginia replied, as she hastily escaped his presence to discuss his request with Mammy.

Mammy replied angrily, "Victor has some nerve to be begging for more soup. Him lucky mi invite him to this party. Him never had enough manners fi say thanks for de food me send fi him the night of the storm."

Virginia's heart skipped a beat as she contemplated the possibility of Mammy confronting Mas Victor about the dinner she was supposed to have taken to him that night. "What if dogs, cats, or mongoose ate the food I left on Mas Victor's doorstep before he opened his door the following morning? What if he saw the food but did not know who left it on his doorstep? What if he said he did not know who left the food? How could I explain why I did not deliver the food to Mas Victor? Could I convince Mammy that I left the food at the door and ran home, because I was afraid of dead people's ghost walking about as duppy at night?"

Virginia quickly suggested, "Mammy, maybe Mas Victor was thinking it was too late to come to our house in the rain just to say thanks when he could do it in the morning. Maybe when the morning come, the thought slipped his mind, because he and everybody else, was swapping stories about the stormy night. Let bygone be bygone. If you have any soup left, pour some in a small cup, and I will see that Lucy give it to him, while I serve the other people."

Virginia's potential crisis momentarily ended when Mammy accepted her explanation. She did not have to explain what she did with the food that night, nor the underlying reasons for her actions. Mammy dished out the soup for Mas Victor, left the kitchen to join those seated in the yard, then addressed them by saying, "I would like to remind you why we are having this celebration. Virginia, come here." In response, Virginia left what she was doing and stood beside her grandmother.

"Standing before all of us today, is a miracle working child of God. What this child did at the beach to save Elder Adams and Sister Mary was a miracle. I knew that she liked going to the beach, but I didn't know that she could swim. I knew she had a good heart, but I didn't know she would risk shark bite or drowning to save, not one but two people. Yes, she proved that God works in mysterious ways, His wonders to perform. After what she did at the beach, she is more than a gift to this family. She is a gift to this district. You now have responsibility to help me raise her. If anybody should hurt one strand of hair on her head, you will answer to me before you answer to God. Hip, hip, hurray!"

At the end of Mammy's speech, everyone sipped whatever was in their cup, while Shut banged the playing cast with newly found zest. But Virginia had mixed emotions about being in the limelight. First, saving those people at the beach was a spontaneous act that still made her tremble in fear when she thinks about it. Second, she felt uncomfortable under the watchful eye of Mas Victor, who may say something unpredictable or demonstrate a willingness to help Mammy raise her.

Elder Adams echoed Mammy's praise of Virginia. "I would not be standing here today if it were not for the miracle that God performed through this virtuous young woman, Virginia. That's why ever since that day at the beach, I have been wondering why God chose her to perform His miracle. Scripture tells us that the disciples were called before they could perform miracles and the more I think about Virginia's life in this district, it's clear to me that God called her a long time ago. She might not have known that God called her. Hallelujah! But look at the evidence. Have you ever seen her gallivanting with idle boys? Have you ever seen or hear her gossiping about other people's business? Have you ever seen or hear of any disobedience to her grandparents? The answer is no to all those questions. Child of God, I give thanks for the blessing you are to this district and pray that your life will be a bright light on the path that other young people will follow to the Lord."

Not to be outdone, Mas Victor stood up unsteadily to add his compliments. His dreadlocks dangled from side to side as he staggered to a nearby tree for support. He had a spliff in one hand and a cup of white rum in the other. "I am the nearest neighbor to Mammy, Tarta, and Virginia. I watch Virginia grow from a pickney to the young woman she is today. I love her like mi own dawta, so if you all don't want no trouble, make sure you no trouble her. That's all mi have fi say."

Virginia was still standing beside Mammy when Mas Victor said, "I love her." Those words broke her concentration and obscured the other words "like mi own dawta" that followed. She had a flashback to that stormy night when he comforted her, and she felt embarrassed that he was announcing his feelings for her to everyone. During the rest of the celebration, she wondered how to relate to Mas Victor after he publicly declared his love for her. But within a few weeks she would be seeking his guidance in answering Mammy's persistent questions about her loss of appetite and frequent vomiting in the mornings.

Neither Virginia nor Mas Victor said much to each other immediately after the celebration hosted by her grandmother, besides casual greetings. She would greet him by saying, "Morning, Mas Victor." He would reply, "Morning, dawta, one love on this beautiful day." But every time she saw him, she reflected on their experience that stormy night.

Daily, she listened to the banter among children her age and older folks for anything reportedly said by Mas Victor about her. But nothing she heard related to the night of the storm. She heard stories about Mas Victor being a "blue foot come from yonder." Some said he came from Kingston "back a wall" where Rasta people live in shacks made of cardboard and other discarded items retrieved from the dunghill. Others said Rasta men from Kingston don't usually work as hard as Mas Victor, so they guessed that he came from a country parish like Manchester or Clarendon.

Mas Victor had no relatives in the district that could be a reference on his early whereabouts. So, the speculations continued while he spent a lot of time socializing at Bulla Shop. One afternoon at the shop, Virginia overheard someone saying that Mas Victor's lover, who'd invited him to move to the district, had left him for another man. Instead of returning to his native parish, he decided to settle down in the house he rented. He worked on the plantations, he smoked weed, and played dominoes every day. He seemed happy, but there were developing concerns that if Mas Victor didn't get his own woman soon, he could start lusting after someone else's woman, in ways that would lead to disastrous results.

Virginia empathized with Mas Victor's plight, but she wondered if he had a secret lover that escaped the notice of everyone. Could he be doing more than lusting after other women in the district? She reached deep into her memory bank to recall evidence of women who visited Mas Victor while she was at home. When she could not recall any, she wondered if his encounters occurred while she was at school. But she quickly discounted that idea, because Mas Victor kept himself busy at work during the day. Although she could not identify any woman in the district who was visiting Mas Victor, she told herself that he may have had encounters late at night and the women left before daylight.

At the end of each day Virginia was left with intense desire to get answers to unanswered questions about Mas Victor. She often went to bed with Mas Victor on her mind, and sometimes she woke up in the mornings nauseous after a night of worrying. In fact, she became so nauseous one morning that she vomited. The second time she was vomiting by the side of the house, Mammy overheard the heaving and inquired, "What did you eat last night that upset you stomach? I wonder if you a get di flu?"

Mammy's questions did not require a verbal answer from Virginia, but they left Virginia guessing about the reason for her sickness. It was jackfruit season and Virginia had eaten a large slice of jackfruit before going to bed, but if that had made her sick it would be an unusual experience, because she ate jackfruit many times in the past without vomiting. Throughout the day Virginia felt listless and barely interested in eating, so Mammy gave her some hot fever grass tea and told her to rest in the shade of a large mango tree. She showed little improvement during the rest of the day. She did not eat the fish soup dinner and went to bed without complaining of hunger.

On the third day of this episodic vomiting, Mammy remembered not seeing sanitary napkins hanging on the clothesline to dry. It was the time of month to see the napkins on the line. So, she asked Virginia if she had missed her period. Virginia responded that it was not time for her period. But Mammy began to wonder if the devil had showed his serpent head to her granddaughter. After she reflected on Mammy's question, Virginia began to wonder if her period was late and if that one incident with Mas Victor could have resulted in her being in the family's way. So, she planned to have a conversation with Mas Victor that evening. She slipped away from home and quietly knocked on Mas Victor's door. The scent of ganja greeted her before Mas Victor did. He welcomed her with both words and gestures into his house, after briefly looking at the neighboring houses to be sure no one was watching her enter his house.

"Do you need some more matches to light the fire tomorrow?" Mas Victor asked.

"No, Mas Victor," she replied.

"So, what do my little dawta need tonight?"

She replied, "I have something very private to talk about, and I feel ashamed to talk to anyone about it but you."

"Okay, I'm all ears. Talk to me, dawta," said Mas Victor, as he reclined in a chair to listen.

"A few days ago, I started vomiting in the morning and feeling sick during the day. Mammy gave me homemade medicine, but it didn't make mi feel any better. Then Mammy asked me if I missed my period. I told her it was not that time of the month, because I couldn't think of a reason for my period to be late. But now that Mammy brought it to my attention, I am wondering if what you did to me that stormy night made me pregnant?"

"Dawta, what did I-man do to you?" Mas Victor asked. "Rain drench you. You were dripping wet. I sheltered you and give you something fi drink till the storm end and you could go back home safely."

"Yes, Mas Victor, you did all that, but when we were frightened by the thunder and lightning, you tried to offer me more protection. You held me very close. I felt you trembling when you lost your balance, fell on the ground with me lying on top of you. I was wondering if I was too heavy to be lying on top of you, but I couldn't move even if I wanted to, because your arms were holding me so tight. I tried to relax by imagining that I was a chicken under the protected wings of a mother hen."

"True word, dawta! That sounds like something I-man would do for the daughters of Zion," he responded.

"But, Mas Victor, that was not all that you did. It's the other things that you did that is causing me to worry. So, I am asking you if you believe those other things you did to me are preventing me from having my period?"

"Now, dawta, tell I-man di truut, was dat di first time a puppy slip inna de pum-pum door?"

"Yes, Mas Victor."

"But after di likkle door open, how many more puppy yuh rescue?" he asked.

"I never did it with anyone else, before or after you. That's why I came to you for help, because I don't know what to do if I am pregnant."

"Dawta, dis modern Babylon is a difficult place for the children of Africa, including you, me, and any pickney you birth in this land. The first thing will happen to I. Dem wi drive I out a di district before daylight if word spread that mi turn yu inna baby madda. So, nobody haffi know nothing til I figure out what to do."

"But what do I say to Mammy?" Virginia asked.

"Tell her that you think di excitement at di beach disturb your system and delayed your period."

Although Mas Victor did not offer any valuable solution to Virginia's question, he gave her a temporary plan to keep Mammy off guard for a few days. Virginia hurried back home before anyone discovered that she had visited Mas Victor. In the next two weeks, Virginia's morning sickness continued unabated, despite the home-made medicine that Mammy gave her.

"Virginia, I don't know if you picked up a new sickness, and I don't know what damage it is doing inside your body to cause the constant vomiting and loss of appetite. So, I think it is a good idea to have a doctor examine you and give you the right medicine. In the morning, I'm taking you to see Dr. Lucas," Mammy announced.

During the remaining hours of that day, Virginia prayed for a miracle that would stop her vomiting and start her menstrual cycle. But no miracle occurred. She was ambivalent about the anticipated findings by the doctor. If he discovered a new sickness, will he find a cure? If he failed, how much longer will she have to suffer? If she is pregnant, how will she explain having sex with Mas Victor in a way that won't cause trouble for her and for him? What will Mammy and Tarta do to her?

The first visit to Dr. Lucas did not scare her as she feared. His reception area had only a few people waiting, and she did not have to wait a long time to see him. While waiting, she amused herself by looking at wall decorations, which included pictures of people on beaches and fat cows in a pasture. But she had a more somber countenance while listening to conversations by other patients waiting to see the doctor. One woman expressed concern that little Johnny refused to eat because his throat hurt him even if he swallowed water. She believed Dr. Lucas will have to remove his tonsils.

The man nearest to Mammy on the bench gasped for air when he breathed. The woman who accompanied him said he had bronchitis. Sitting opposite that woman, a young girl shivered with ague. Her mother speculated that the girl contracted malaria fever.

As Mammy watched Virginia's countenance changed by those sad stories, she comforted her granddaughter by holding her hand.

The nurse escorted Mammy and Virginia from the waiting area to the doctor's office. "My name is Dr. Lucas. What's your name, young lady?" he introduced himself.

"My name is Virginia, sir," she replied.

He asked a few questions about how long she had been ill, and what she had been eating, before saying, "When you return home, please be careful not to drink the river water that looks like oil is floating on it. Sanitary inspectors have been spraying oil-based chemicals in the river to kill mosquito larvae. Some people try to skim the oil off the water before filling their buckets. But enough contaminants remain in the water to make them sick. I will check to see if that problem made you sick. Please open your mouth. Stick out your tongue! Say ah-ah-ah-ah! I will use this little instrument to examine your ears. Turn your head to the right. Now to the left. I will have the nurse take your blood and urine samples. She will also make an appointment for a return visit, possibly next Monday."

There was not much discussion about the doctor's visit on the way home. But Virginia could hardly wait to tell Mas Victor what the doctor said about the possible relationship between her illness and the contaminated drinking water from the river. But while she processed that thought, she questioned herself why no one else in the household was vomiting each morning even though they drank the same river water.

Virginia waited until evening shadows gave her cover to slip over to Mas Victor's house with news of the doctor's visit. But when she knocked on the door, he did not answer. She felt disappointed, but she thought he may be playing dominoes at Bulla Shop. She would not try to see him again until the following week.

When Virginia returned to Dr. Lucas for the lab results, he asked Mammy to remain in the waiting room while he examined Virginia. He quickly determined that her temperature and heart rate were normal. But there was a reason for her morning sickness that had nothing to do with the water she drank.

The doctor explained his diagnosis by saying, "Virginia, the test results indicate the reason for your vomiting and loss of appetite. You do not have a deadly disease. That's one good news. The other is that you are in the family's way, and if you are fortunate, the morning sickness will end in about two months. I anticipate Mammy will be surprised to hear the news and will want to know about the baby father and his plans for you and the baby. I will do my best to ensure that you have a healthy baby. So, I would like to see you monthly to monitor the development of the baby. Now, do you want me to break the news to Mammy? Or do you want to tell her yourself?"

There was a long pause before Virginia's words followed the tears that began to trickle down her cheeks. "Are you sure that I'm pregnant, Doctor Lucas?" But before the doctor could reply to her question, Virginia continued to mumble, "Mammy and Tarta are going to be ashamed of me and they are going to be mad with Mas Victor."

"Why will she be angry with Mas Victor?" the doctor asked.

"Because he is the father of the baby, if I am pregnant. They will blame him for taking advantage of me and that will make him the most unpopular man in the district. They might even beat him to death and leave my baby without a father."

"If you have those concerns, I will start the conversation with Mammy before you leave my office," the doctor said.

When Mammy entered the doctor's office, she quickly observed tears flowing down Virginia's cheeks. She hugged her granddaughter and assured her that not all sickness result in death. "Even if you got bad news from Doctor Luke, you have experienced the miracle working power of God at the beach and know that God is a present help in times of trouble."

"This is not a sickness that results in death. This sickness is the result of new life. Virginia is pregnant," the doctor said.

Mammy loosened her hug of Virginia as the doctor's words sank into her consciousness. "So, the vomiting and loss of appetite is really morning sickness?" Mammy asked.

"Correct!" said the doctor.

"So, who is the faada? I never saw nor heard that you were flirting with any of those lazy good-for-nothing boys in the district. You were always home, except when you went to school or the beach. When and where could this happen to you?"

"Mammy, I did not try to do anything wrong. I couldn't find any matches to light the fire before you and Tarta came home from the field that stormy night, so I went to Mas Victor's house to ask him for matches, as I did many times before. The difference this time was the sudden storm that wet me up and forced me to shelter in his house. I was soaking wet by the time he opened his door and let me in. He sent me into his back room to wring the water out of my clothes. He even took off his shirt and allowed me to wear it while my wet clothes were drying. I was half naked and frightened by the lightning when Mas Victor tried to comfort me like a mother hen. He fell, and I fell on top of him. He held me so close to him for such a long time like a protective mother hen, until I almost fell asleep. I never had sex with anyone else and felt ashamed after it happened. I was still trembling with fear when you and Tarta came home from the field, but I did not mention what had just happened to me. If I did find the matches in the kitchen to light the fire before you came home from the field, I would not have gone to Mas Victor and end up being pregnant now."

"Virginia, I always knew you were a good girl, and I don't blame you for trying to do what you always did in the evenings—start the fire for me to start cooking dinner as soon as possible after me and Tarta come home from the field. But I can't excuse Victor's slack behavior. He is a grown man and you are a child who was in distress. You needed a lifeline, not his big dirty Rasta man cock. I thank you, Doctor, for your medical service. We have a long road ahead, and I pray that God will be our pilot."

On the way home, both Virginia and Mammy were silent, except for the two or three times that Mammy muttered that in some foreign countries, Victor would be arrested for rape and sentenced to prison. One would think the first thing Mammy did when she reached home was to break the news of Virginia's pregnancy to Tarta. But she did not. Instead, she went knocking on Victor's door, while Virginia braced herself for a fiery confrontation. There was no response from Victor. The ritual of knocking on Victor's door at various times of day continued for three days without any response. By then Mammy notified Tarta, who prepared for the confrontation by sharpening his machete that he normally used to cut logwood. Fueled by anger and frustration, Mammy started inquiring about Victor's whereabouts when she spoke to next door neighbors or those she encountered at the Bulla Shop where Victor usually played dominoes.

Although Victor's playing partners had not seen him for nearly a week, his absence was considered unusual, but not alarming. So, no one went looking for him. But now that Mammy, his immediate neighbor, was inquiring about him, word quickly spread that Victor was missing. Various people speculated about what may have happened to him. He may have been injured in the field and could not make it home? He may be in jail on a ganja charge? He may have found another woman with whom he is having a blissful honeymoon and did not want to be disturbed?

Finally, Mammy contacted Johnny, who owns the house that Victor rented. But since Victor paid his last rent, Johnny had not heard from him. He speculated that Victor might have gone to some Rasta meeting, got high and was chilling with his brethren. Amidst all the uncertainty, Mammy posed a question to Johnny, "What if he is dead in the house? One sure way of answering that question is if someone with keys to the house opens the door and verify whether or not he is in the house."

Although Johnny was reluctant at first to invade Victor's privacy, he couldn't bear the thought of anyone finding Victor's rotting body in his house. He agreed to open the door that evening if Victor was not seen by 6:00 PM.

Bang! Bang! Bang! Johnny knocked on the door. But no response. Johnny tried to open the door, but his key did not fit the lock. He could not hide his surprised that Victor changed the lock without notifying him. When he succeeded in breaking that lock, he discovered that the door had an additional dead bolt on the inside of the house that prevented him from opening the door from the outside. His surprise turned to anger, because Victor did not consult him before installing two unauthorized locks on the door.

But while Johnny's anger was simmering and about to erupt, he had immediate concerns about the implication of Victor's death in the house. The dead bolt signifies that someone is locked inside. What if Victor died in the house? He had no known relatives in the district, so who would be responsible for his funeral? Who will rent the house if people knew that someone died in the house and if they believed it could be haunted by the spirit of a Rasta man?

Mammy had different concerns about Victor's absence. Privately she believed that Victor deserved to die, but she would not be consoled by his premature death. She mumbled softly to Tarta, "He left my granddaughter with a rotten seed growing in her belly and when the child is born, she will have to raise that child without the support of a father."

"What if he did not die of natural causes, but that someone broke in the house and killed him?" Johnny wondered loudly. "I will check the windows to see if any of them is open." Shortly after, Johnny found the back window open. He crawled into the house and discovered to his relief that Victor had left. He took most of his clothes and did not vandalize the house. Johnny walked to the front door, unbolted it and confirmed to Mammy and Tarta that Victor was not in the house.

Mammy returned to her house. She informed Virginia that Victor vanished, but left no forwarding address. Virginia received the news with mixed feelings of disappointment and relief. She felt relief that the anticipated bloodshed had been averted, but she also felt disappointed that Victor left her without any emotional or financial support during her pregnancy. She concluded that after she told him about her symptoms, he anticipated the results from the doctor and then abandoned her.

News about Virginia's pregnancy started to spread slowly through the district, but no one correctly guessed the identity of the child's father. The news also spread to her best friend, Lucy, who missed her at school and tried unsuccessfully to persuade Virginia to join her at the beach where they often socialized.

Lucy visited Virginia at home and became the first person outside the immediate family to be told about the pregnancy and the challenges ahead. Virginia told her about the morning sickness, the suspense during the doctor's visit, Mammy's disappointment, and the mystery of Mas Victor's disappearance. Both girls wept as Lucy consoled her friend.

Elder Adams also heard about the pregnancy and directed his wrathful prayers against Victor as the devil incarnate. He also led an effort to support Virginia and her unborn child. He was determined to prove that God can right any wrong.

Virginia reflected on the relationship between a pair of turtle doves that her grandparents kept as pets. They demonstrated their love for each other by constant communication with each other through a range of sounds. They preened each other's feathers and the male frequently kissed the female when he inserted food into her mouth.

Unlike those birds, there was no prolonged courtship between her and Victor that modeled the relationship she admired. There was no friendship that exemplified her grandparents' relationship. Her relationship with Victor was almost like animals grazing in the same pasture. They saw each other in passing from one location to another, with no special attention until the female was in heat. Unlike the animals, she gave no signal that she was in heat. But he acted like a wild boar hog that forced its screw-like penis into a virginal piglet. He then abandoned her and his child to wallow in the mud he left behind as his ironic consolation.

Except for the morning sickness which lasted about three months, Virginia's pregnancy was otherwise uneventful. She named her son Harry Victor at birth.

Occasionally, during the pregnancy and after the birth of Harry, Virginia receive an envelope at the post office addressed to her. The envelopes had no sender's name nor address. The sending post office varied among different parishes. Rather than writing letters, the sender folded paper money in blank sheets of paper, addressed the envelope to Virginia, before mailing the letter. The money varied between one and two pounds sterling each time. Both Mammy and Virginia speculated that Victor was the person sending the anonymous letters in acknowledgement of his guilt. They also wished that his conscience continued to prick him for the rest of his life.

Just as Mammy and Tarta were adjusting to their new life with Virginia and her baby, Mammy suddenly became ill and died. There were no warning signs. She had gone to prayer meeting the Wednesday night and testified about God's goodness to her and her family. She thanked God that Virginia gave birth to a healthy boy who will not be influenced by his good-for-nothing daddy. She prayed for long life to witness God's blessings on the third and fourth generations of her family.

"We returned home from church and went to bed," Tarta recalled, "then during the night, heavy shaking of the bed wake mi up. The shaking was like earthquake. Strange thing was that the terrible shaking did not wake up Mammy. She was still fast asleep like a baby. I come off the bed, lite the lamp, and I saw with my two eyes that Mammy's whole body was shaking. I tried to wake her up from what I consider a bad dream, but she never responded. I pulled back her eyelids, but they quickly closed as soon as I released them. In desperation I shouted for help from her dearly departed mother rather than God who seemed so far away. I said, 'Mama Jones, I know you keep watch over your beloved daughter all the time, even now when Satan is shaking the life out of her. She is tired, but not ready for eternal rest, so wake her up to enjoy your gift of baby Harry.'

"She stopped shaking. So, I held my eyeglasses under her nose for about a minute to see if her breath would fog up my glasses, but she did not breathe. Although I did not want to wake up the baby, I called out to Virginia in the other room, where they were sleeping. She rushed in to discover what I refused to admit, even though Mammy was lying still with froth on her lips. Mammy is dead."

Mammy's funeral procedures were typical of the period in Plantation Valley. The body was iced in the house with large blocks of ice for two days, while friends made the coffin from crude lumber and dug the grave in the backyard with zest influenced by white rum. Relatives and friends gathered in the yard of the deceased each day and night for nine days to comfort the grieving family with food, drinks, and shared memories of the deceased.

But Mammy had to be buried before the third day after her death, to prevent her spirit from leaving her body to reside in the house, possibly haunting its occupants. So, at the end of the second day, Elder Adams presided over her funeral service.

He acknowledged Tarta and other family members. He welcomed friends and neighbors, before inviting everyone to sing Mammy's favorite hymn.

"Jesus, lover of my soul,
Let me to Thy bosom fly,
While the nearer waters roll,
While the tempest still is high:

Hide me, O my Savior, hide,
Till the storm of life is past;
Safe into the haven guide;
O receive my soul at last."

After the hymn, the Elder granted Tarta's wish to pay tribute to his dearly departed wife. Tarta said tearfully, "Mammy was my bosom friend from the time me and her were teenagers. We stop attending school early in life to work long side our parents in the fields. By the time we moved in together, she knew how to stretch the little we earned like elastic bands around the things we buy. We did not have much materially, but we did not feel dirt poor, because we use to see people less thrifty than us, struggling to feed their families with empty hands. At five feet six inches she was average height of women in the district. Her tight body was true testimony to her hard work. But the softness of her sunflower smile was often reflected on people's faces when she greeted them. She was a friend to every God-fearing person, but enemy to no one. Mammy, you will continue to be my morning star. May you rest in peace forever."

After a few more tributes, Elder Adams thanked God for the faithfulness of the dearly departed and the legacy of goodwill her family inherited. He completed the burial ritual with the words, "Ashes to ashes, dust to dust," while the burial attendants lowered her coffin in the grave.

Tarta's closest friends left the grave site to rearrange the furniture in the house. They disassembled the bed before leaning it against the wall. They placed tables and chairs in different locations, presumably to confuse Mammy's departed spirit that may be reluctant to leave the house.

Mourning continued for seven more days until the special nine-night ceremony, which freed Mammy's dead spirit to roam far away from the home. Key elements of that night were the Kumina music, dancing, drinking, especially over-proof white rum, eating roasted and curried meats with roasted breadfruit. If breadfruits were not in season, white rice would be cooked without salt and served as a substitute. No one ate before Tarta took a portion of the food to the grave sites of Mammy's departed relatives. Following the ritual of serving food to the dead, the ceremony continued with hymn singing, led by someone reciting words of the songs for others to follow; energetic drumming by men who sat facing each other on the playing cyas and the bandu drums. People shuffle-danced around the drummers, some in a Myalism trance, while mingling with spirits of the ancestors.

Shut, sitting on the playing cyas drum, showed the first evidence of being possessed by spirits of the departed. He fell to the ground, his body shaking like someone who had epileptic seizure. He shouted in an alien language, barely recognizable by anyone, "Brakish wata! Brakish wata!"

In response, someone gave him white rum in a glass. He gulped down the rum, bit off a piece of the glass, chewed it without any obvious cuts or blood in his mouth. The astonished looked on as he tossed the remaining portion of the glass toward the grave, climb a nearby calabash tree, hung upside down with only his feet clinging to a branch. He continued to shout, "Brakis wata! Brakish wata!"

Shut's frenzy soon spread among other dancers, including women who convulsed under the Myal spell. Many spoke in unknown tongues as they fell on the ground. Mesmerized onlookers heard the unintelligible sounds and guttural utterances. But unlike experiences on the Day of Pentecost, most listeners did not understand the utterances shouted by those possessed of the spirits.

The ceremony ended after midnight. The weary went home to rest. But they set Mammy free to continue her journey away from the home, in the fellowship of other departed souls.

CHAPTER 5

Business Motherhood Competition

Virginia's life changed significantly after Mammy's death. She had to do more than the morning chores and lighting fire to cook the evening meals. Now she cooked most meals and performed housekeeping duties while caring for her infant son, Harry. Those daily challenges were complicated by scarcity of money.

Tarta earned some cash working in the sugarcane field during sugar harvesting season, between June and December. His work week was four days, with eight hours considered a full day. He also had to make time to work on the rented farm, where he planted and harvested crops to feed the family. He no longer had the support of Mammy's help.

Driven by her Scorpio personality to seek financial success, Virginia began supplementing the family's income by boiling and selling coconut oil. She purchased fifty coconuts from surrounding residents, shelled and grated them before washing the fibers to extract the milk. She boiled the milk to separate oil from the custard-like residue. Usually, fifty coconuts produced four quarts of oil, which she sold to families in the district. Within weeks of that business adventure, she purchased increased number of coconuts and had to hire a few helpers to produce the oil. But with the additional coconuts, she produced more oil than people in the district needed. To solve the overproduction problem, she sold the excess oil on Saturdays, in the nearest town market five miles from home.

After selling in the local market a few weeks, she heard that people in Kingston paid a higher price for oil than people in the country. That information prompted her to develop strategies to profit from that opportunity. They included production of enough oil to offset the costs of additional workers, larger storage, portable containers, round trip to Kingston and possible overnight stay, if all the oil were not sold in a day.

By her calculation, she needed to produce an additional four gallons of oil each week for the Kingston market. But that could be done only if she had reliable supplies of no less than two hundred and fifty coconuts each week. She assumed that her local sources for fifty coconuts were reliable. Her challenge was to find sources for the other two hundred. She discussed her concerns with Tarta and sought advice, "Tarta, people say that I can make more money selling the coconut oil in Coronation Market. Where do you think I can get more coconuts on a regular basis to make five gallons of oil to sell in Kingston each week?"

Tarta thought for a while about legitimate sources for the coconuts, but concluded in his mind that there were none, except the plantation owners. "Virginia, my mind landed on the Backra man them as your only large suppliers, because they grow most of the coconuts. But they use all their coconuts to make products, some of which they export to other countries like Britain. If we had to get coconuts from them, it would not be by asking. We would have to take it, or have it taken on a weekly basis. It will be risky, but I will do whatever I can to make sure you succeed in your business."

After their discussion Tarta began networking with enterprising estate employees and their unemployed counterparts to supply two hundred coconuts, illicitly harvested from the surrounding plantations. With increased supply of coconuts, Virginia recruited additional helpers to produce the coconut oil. In addition to shelling and grating the coconuts, some drew several buckets of water from a nearby spring to wash the milk from the grated coconuts. Others gathered and delivered a steady supply of firewood to boil the coconut oil. Those were daunting challenges, but Virginia was determined to close the financial gap left by both Mammy and Mas Victor.

Although the coconut oil business consumed most of her time, Harry was always in the back of her mind. She fed, bathed, and dressed him in the mornings, but hardly had time to interact with him during the remaining hours of the day. Eventually, she entrusted the responsibilities of feeding him and changing his clothes to various workers and friends. She had no consistent babysitter for him while at home or when delayed in Kingston for a day or two. Eventually there was an inverse relationship between caring for Harry and her devotion to the business.

Tarta watched in silence the increasing emotional distance between Virginia and her son. He shared Harry's suffering as the child's emotional behavior gradually changed from clay-like stability to quicksand, in response to his mother's distant and less predictable behavior. But the most impactful incident was the fowl incident in the kitchen.

Harry was a five-year-old boy, playfully feeding a hen and her five chickens in the yard, near the right side of the house. He held a small bowl of dried corn in his outstretched right hand to feed the birds. When they abruptly walked away because their crops were full, he misunderstood the reason why they walked away. He thought they no longer wanted to play with him. Acting on his assumption, he followed them with the bowl and tried to entice them with the feed by repeating, "Chick, chick, chick, here's your corn. Chick, chick, chick, here's your corn." When the chickens turned deaf ears to his pleas by running away, their inaudible resolution said, "Mi no want no corn."

Harry redoubled his efforts. "Chick, chick, you didn't finish your food." But the mother hen and her chickens ran away from him at increased speed, with him in pursuit. Mother hen ran into the kitchen, followed by her chickens. Harry followed closely behind them. In desperation the hen flew onto the kitchen counter and accidentally overturned several dishes with the evening meal Virginia had just prepared. In fairness to Harry, he never intended to play with the chickens in the kitchen. He was content to play with them in the yard, where he was feeding them. They ran away from him, only to be trapped in the kitchen. In a panic, the mother hen flew rather than run out of the kitchen. Harry did not anticipate the hen's flight. He did not foresee nor control the damage she would cause.

Virginia took none of Harry's perspective into consideration. Following the crash of dishes and kitchen utensils, Harry heard his mother, shouting to a God who may have been deaf. "Oh God, you gave me a child, but he is growing into a monster. The minute I take my eyes off him, he runs into trouble. You know how hard I worked to prepare dinner for the family, but because of Harry, the dogs will be fed instead. In the name of God the Father, God the Son, and God the Holy Ghost, please have mercy on me today. If it's your will that I succeed with this new business, please calm the spirit of Satan in this child before he drives me mad! Slow down this cursed child to crawl like a sloth rather than run into any more trouble!"

After she spoke to God, she angrily ordered Harry to bed, much earlier than bedtime. "Harry, go to your bed at once! I don't care whether you want to sleep. Just don't leave the bed before I call you!"

Her punishment was very severe and probably inappropriate for a playful child. No one had ever heard her say a harsh word to anyone before, even though harsh words were routinely spoken by people in the community. Additionally, no one at that time anticipated the prolonged mental and physical effects of her "slow him down" curse on her infant son, Harry.

Virginia's distance from her son, while being attentive to everything and everyone, triggered Harry's increased emotional hunger for her. Pain of that hunger was no different from pain felt by a starving child watching everyone else being fed in a family owned restaurant. Additionally, small fractions of attention from indifferent women assigned to mother him guaranteed that he was not emotionally attached to anyone, not even his mother. So, the word mamma did not have the same emotional significance to him as it did to the other children he grew up with. His mother's unplanned neglect was compounded by the fact that he never met his father, nor had the opportunity to call someone Papa, like the other children in the district called their father. Tarta was both grandfather and substitute father, but saying Tarta did not satisfy his emotional longing to say Papa like other children.

Although Tarta did not satisfy Harry's emotional need for a father, he offered him contentment by telling his great-grandson fascinating stories about notable dead people, especially those who were Maroons. Folk tales about less notable people included variation of three ghost stories. One dealt with ghosts invading dreams of sleeping adults as prophets to warn of future danger. Ghosts in another variation, kept watchful eyes on children and reported misdeeds to parents in dreams. In the third variation, ghosts invaded people's dreams to issue threats of deaths or bodily harm. Ghosts in Tarta's wakeful and dream stories often disguise themselves as birds, particularly black birds and ground doves. They live among people. In an amusing story, a black bird invaded Tarta's dream with a warning for a parent. "Warn Rude Boy Rudy's muma and pupa that me almost lost mi temper and hurt them son yesterday, when him fling stone and broke my eyeglasses." Tarta chuckled in his dream when he reflected on the ghost wearing glasses. The ghost continued, "Don't laugh like I am giving you joke! This is serious. Before I turn duppy, I used to have fun at Bulla Shop, so I still hang out on the overhead electric wires sometimes, to catch up on the latest gossip. That Rude Boy shouldn't fling stone at every bird him see, because him no know which bird is real. Him shouldn't break me glasses, when mi no do him nothing. So, tell him parents say, I can't promise to forgive him if him do it again. They must teach him to expect double trouble, if him troubled, trouble that didn't trouble him."

Tarta told Harry about old people's beliefs about ground doves that spend more time walking around in cemeteries than flying or perched in trees, because they were weighed down by good or bad dead people spirits living in them. Since no one knew which bird had good or bad spirit, people didn't throw stones at any ground doves. He told other interesting stories about Maroons who were his and Harry's ancestors. They were men and women captured in Africa by white people and brought to Jamaica as slaves. After a while, those men and women decided that they would no longer endure the hardship of slavery. They began to challenge slave masters until they successfully defended themselves against cruel white people. They were so very sensitive to one another's spirits that Maroons, a hundred miles away, could send and receive messages with the aid of a modified conch shell called an abeng. But people who were not Maroons could not interpret those messages, even if they heard the sounds. The abeng was also used as a siren. A maroon would blow the abeng from the top of a hill in the district on Banana-Days to notify people that a cargo ship was in port to be loaded with bananas for shipment to England. Additionally, the siren gave people two opportunities. Some would seek work at the pier. Others would quickly harvest their bananas and try to sell them at the wharf before the boat departed.

Two of Tarta's favorite Maroons stories were about a woman named Nanny and a man named Paul Bogle. Tarta loved Nanny because she protected the Maroons in Portland from cruelty by white slave owners. A British soldier said to her, "Nanny, I believe you want to live in peace just as we do, but I understand that your soldiers are making unreasonable demands that you keep on fighting for peace. People in Britain, where I come from, find the idea 'fighting for peace' ironic, that is not sincere. For us peace is a gift from each side to the other, as a sign of friendship. If you agree with me, I will help you achieve peace the British way, by getting rid of the people who are impediments to peace."

Nanny quietly asked, "How will you get rid of my people who are impediments?" She asked that question because she wasn't sure if she understood his big words.

"First, you will round them up in a special location, then you invite us to do the negotiation with them on your behalf. We will give them their right to live in peace if they continue to be productive workers on the plantations. Those who agree will be separated from others who don't accept our gift. Those who disagree will have to be silenced by you or by us."

Nanny agreed to call the meeting and present the British request to her Maroon people. But she and her people understood that if they were unarmed when they met armed British soldiers, the only gift they would receive was death. She did not follow the agreed plan.

She tricked the British soldiers into believing she went further than the agreed plan. "Many of my soldiers did not agree with that plan. They were so angry with me that they threatened to kill me. I had to act quickly to put down their rebellion by killing those who threatened me and the peaceful settlement with British people."

She convinced the soldiers with both the story she told them and the fresh blood she showed them on the pathway to the place where the Maroons lived. But unknown to the soldiers, the blood was from goats Nanny killed earlier. They were also convinced that Nanny no longer had a fighting army of Maroons. They decided to advance on the settlement and force Nanny to surrender, but she surprised them by calling her soldiers out from hiding in the bushes to ambush and kill the British soldiers.

Tarta told Harry, "That long-ago victory remains one of the most important victories of Black people against British soldiers in Jamaica. It resulted in Maroon's freedom from white man's authority and Maroon's freedom to manage their lives. Their slavery ended nearly a hundred years ahead of other Black people in Jamaica."

Tarta's next story was about his other hero, Paul Bogle, who lived right there in the parish of St. Thomas, next door to Portland. "There were two important differences between Paul and Nanny, besides the fact that he was a man and she was a woman. First, he fought openly, not secretly, against rich white people, including the high-ranking governor of the island. He fought to secure Black people's rights, thirty years after slavery was officially abolished. His fight was not limited to a local area like Nanny Town in Portland, but wherever the injustice existed in the island. Second, while Nanny fought to break the physical chains of slavery, Paul fought to break the white man's invisible slave chains, because that type of slavery had not been abolished.

"How did Mr. Paul Bogle see the invisible chains, Tarta?" Harry asked.

Tarta replied, "Only a smart Maroon would ask that question at such a young age. The invisible chains are like invisible wind. Even though we can't see the wind, we can feel its effects that are sometimes strong enough to blow down trees in a hurricane. Mr. Bogle saw the effects of those invisible chains, just as clearly as we see the effects of a hurricane. White people used two types of chains to keep Black people in slavery. One type was made of iron attached to their hands, their feet, and around their waists. That type of chain was visible and outlawed. The chains Bogle was trying to break were stronger than iron, even though they were invisible in people's brains. People suffering the effects of that type of slavery either see the world through their slave masters' eyes, or through their own cross eyes. Those who see the world through the eyes of their slave masters are less rebellious against the oppression. Those with cross eyes don't focus on their plight. They are like little Johnny, who lives at Top Land. He always seems to be walking in a direction different from where he is looking. You may even know children who make fun of him by saying, 'Look where you are going, or go where you are looking.'

"But real Maroons in Plantation district can see that Black people are invisibly chained to their tiny huts, unable to move to other locations, while white people continue to live in big houses anywhere they choose to live. Those invisible chains keep Black people working long hours in the sun, for very little money, while white people sit in the shade and get rich. Nanny had already broken the visible iron chains of slavery for some people. Paul was trying to break the invisible chain in people's head. It required a different kind of instrument than the machete Nanny used. His invisible instrument was not sharp enough to chop through the invisible chains at that time. White people hanged him in Morant Bay for attempting to break those chains and they will continue to kill Black people who are determined to break invisible chains." Tarta concluded the story by telling Harry, "Many people continue to mourn Bogle's death, but all living Maroons know that his death was not in vain. He died trying to save Black people. Hopefully when you grow up, you will also be able to see the invisible chains and invent ways to break them."

In addition to his favorite heroes, Nanny and Paul Bogle, Tarta told Harry about another Maroon fighter named Dutty Boukman. "He was white people's slave in Jamaica and later in an island called Haiti. While in Haiti, Boukman organized other slaves to rebel against white French slave owners. He was killed publicly like Paul

Bogle. But the revolution he started continued after his death and was successful under the leadership of a Black man named Toussaint Louverture."

By the time Harry started school, images of Tarta's stories filled his brain. He wished they were also in the school books. Reading pictorial stories of rabbits, chickens, and British plants did not seem interesting as the stories he heard at home about Breda Anancy. Unlike the language spoken at home, school book stories were written in a language he did not speak. The word he knew as Mada became mother; fada became father; sista became sister; breda became brother. There were stories about roosters making lots of noise by crowing early mornings, with the accuracy of an alarm clock to wake everyone to the dawning of a new day. But there was no story about hens laying eggs in their nests and immediately announcing the event to their rooster companion, with the cackle, "Cock, cock, cock me layo."

The books presented a funny Breda Rabbit, but in those stories he was not as smart nor as mysterious as the stories Tarta told him at home about a spider, that people called Breda Anancy, or Breda Nancy, when they shorten his name. Breda Rabbit's big trick was the way he built his house to escape mongoose, snakes, and other enemies. The underground house had several entrances and Rabbit loved to tell how he confused his enemies with hide-go-seek games of slipping in and out of various entrances. Breda Nancy survived with many more tricks. First, he was a mixture of the living and the dead. No one knew his parents nor his birthday, although it was widely believed that he was born near the end of the week. He was small in comparison to other animals but survived by being smarter than them. He could walk or float in the air like a kite, using multipurpose threads he made in his body. He also made webs with the threads that served as a house for his family and a trap for enemies including flies, bees, mosquitos, and other insects which his family ate. Long ago in Africa, Nancy taught Maroons how to knit fish nets like a spider web and use them to catch fish in the sea. Maroons in Jamaica were still using knitted fish nets to catch fish.

Although Nancy was a good provider for his family, he played tricks on them sometimes, just as he did to other animals. He even changed into other creatures that his family did not recognize. One day, he changed into a dove that brought home four ripe plums for his wife and three children. He gave a plum to each of them. When they began to eat their plums and saw that he had nothing to eat, each of them gave him half a plumb. That resulted in him eating two plums, but more importantly, he proved that his family loved him.

As Harry grew older, school became less interesting, partly because of his teachers' negative interactions with him and other students in school. They used to beat him with switches and leather straps when he did not do or say what they wanted. There was very little to laugh about, except when students were secretly being mischievous, or being mocked for their reaction to punishment by the teachers. One of his funniest experiences in school was an incident involving Mr. Whitelock, the inspector of schools, and a girl named Maybie. Whitelock was sent by the government to determine how well students were doing in school, by their individual answers to his various questions. Although Harry did not remember Whitelock's question nor Maybie's answer, he could not forget Whitelock's insulting response after Maybie stood up and nervously said something in response to his question.

Whitelock shouted, "Sit down, you nincompoop!"

Harry had never heard that word nincompoop before, but thought from the sound of it, that Whitelock was accusing her of passing gas, publicly pooping in the class. There was no foul smell, but the entire class reacted to the insult the same way. They laughed mockingly at Maybie for what was thought to be her inappropriate behavior. During the prolonged laughter, Maybie shamefully picked up her books and left the class crying. She never returned to school. But even worse, no one challenged Whitelock's behavior and his impact on children the government was paying him to educate.

Meanwhile, Virginia's business required more reliable support than she was receiving from the available pool of workers, so Harry pitched in his help by fetching water from the nearby spring, shelling coconuts, and occasionally accompanying his mother to Coronation Market during school holidays.

Before he went to that market, the busiest place Harry saw was Mr. Main's beehive. Those bees' activities were many and varied. He would have missed significant events had Mr. Main not pointed them out to him. The queen bee was constantly laying eggs; worker bees were being hatched every three days and fed by other bees that acted as nurses. Some mature worker bees were returning to the hive with pollen on their legs and nectar sucked up in their mouths to be turned in to honey. Others made wax cells to store honey for the colony of bees. But their visible activities competed against their buzzes that filled his ears.

Coronation Market was a human beehive. People came from the island's fourteen parishes to sell food products harvested from the fields, household products made from coconut palm, bamboos, and straws. Buyers were people living in the capital city of Kingston. They haggled over prices, while sellers competed against one another to sell their products quickly before the trucks that brought them to the market were ready to return to the country parishes. Harry observed that his mother and few other sellers had regular customers who bought their products quickly. But in the absence of such advantages, sellers fiercely competed by denigrating their competitors' products and promoting their own as superior. He watched a fight between two women after one lured a customer from her competitor.

"Lady, before you buy coconut oil from Portland higglers, you should smell it. It's most likely rancid because they boil the oil long ago and couldn't sell in the country market. If your family eat any food cooked with that oil, you will have no one else to blame when they get sick. Come and taste the difference in my oil that I boiled yesterday."

There was no indication the potential customer confirmed that the accused seller was from Portland or that her oil was rancid; but she walked away and toward the competitor. Before she got to the competitor's stall, the aggrieved seller left her goods unattended, went to the stall of her accuser, violently slapped her face, and spilled her container of oil on the ground.

"You are a lying bitch! Nobody will buy your fresh oil now that I spill it on the ground."

They both wrestled on the oil slick ground, each pulling the other's hair, amidst angry sounds of curse words like fuck, shit, hoar. The market police eventually broke up the fight and expelled both women from the market.

Outside the market Harry saw a tramcar traveling on rail lines buried in the street. It was powered by electricity transmitted through a pole attached to overhead wires. He saw little boys like himself hopping on the tram or hopping off when the conductor was approaching them to collect the fares. He wished that he and his friends in the country had trams to hop on and off during their three-mile hike to and from school each day.

Shortly after his visit to Coronation Market, Virginia expanded her business to include the sale of green bananas. The new venture provided the opportunity for her to buy bananas that were rejected for overseas market at a reduced price and resell them at a profit.

In those days shipping companies bought bananas by the bunch, that is the number of hands on the stems. A bunch had nine hands, three-quarter bunch had eight hands, half a bunch had seven hands, and quarter bunch had six hands. With that classification system, some farmers were selling four six-hand bunches or twenty-four hands of bananas for the same price as a person who sold one bunch with nine hands.

Some farmers had only one stem of banana to sell and carried it on their heads to the wharf. Others with more than one stem relied on donkeys to carry the load to the wharf. Inspectors verified the number of hands and the absence of defects. After the inspection, farmers were paid for the approved bunches. Those that fail the inspection were rejected and returned to the farmers.

In many instances, bananas that failed the test for export market, because of a few bruises on the hands during transportation, would be acceptable for domestic market. But if the domestic market had a glut of perishable bananas for sale, the farmers lost both money and time in the alternative market. Virginia's intervention in buying the rejected bananas at a discount, rescued many farmers from total loss. Additionally, she shifted the glut of bananas from the local market, to the much larger market in Kingston.

That project complemented the coconut oil project at a time when Virginia began to have difficulty getting a reliable supply of coconuts, partly because the trees were dying. Death started slowly. Little coconut blossoms sprouted but faded before they developed into fruits. The palm leaves broke rather than wafted in the wind. Eventually, acres of coconut plantation became a ghostly cemetery of tall leafless trees. No one found the cure for that deadly plant disease.

Following the death of the coconut trees, a second wave of disaster struck. This time it affected the Gross Mitchell bananas, the most lucrative strain of bananas specifically cultivated for overseas market. The fungus affecting the plants were resistant to fungicide. Before the plants died, portions of the leaves became freckled with brown spots that people referred to as leaf spots. The collapse of banana and coconut plantations affected both Virginia and Tarta. She had fewer products to sell in the market and Tarta had less opportunities to work on the large plantation, except in the sugarcane fields. But even that source of employment was threatened when workers on the sugarcane fields went on a prolonged strike for higher wages. Those prevailing circumstances forced Virginia and other villagers to find alternative means of employment.

Some found poorly paid jobs breaking lime stones used to pave Macadamized roadways. Fewer still were employed to drive the tractor that compacted the broken stones. Others were gathering courage to explore opportunities outside Plantation Village.

Just when their hopes were fading, the United States of America began recruiting Jamaican laborers to harvest sugarcane and apples. Their pay may have been lower than their American counterpart, but the prevailing wisdom was that every US dollar they sent home, would be a kind of bonus in Jamaica. Those overseas experiences gave returning farmworkers a different perspective on local plantations and reduced their incentive to resume work in the fields. Those experiences also revived the travel bug spirits of predecessors who improved their families' fortunes by working overseas in Cuba, Panama Canal, and Costa Rica. Britain became an alternative overseas destination for many who did not qualify to enter the US but qualified to enter Britain after serving in the war. Additionally, Britain had become the motherland to Jamaicans after hundreds of years of colonial servitude. Jamaicans were like the proverbial chickens going home to roost in the UK. The primary requirement for a UK passport was a valid birth certificate issued by the government of Jamaica. That requirement was less stringent than getting a visa to the US.

But even that less stringent requirement became a problem for many Jamaicans, including Virginia, whose birth was never registered in the government office. Enterprising Jamaicans quickly took advantage of the business opportunity of expediting the search for birth certificates as go-between the government office and aspiring emigrants, some who were barely literate. Travel agents competed for clients among themselves and against less reliable expediters, by offering extra services, including applying for clients' birth certificates and finding residence in England, allegedly at no extra cost. Virginia took advantage of the travel agents' more reliable services and applied for her passport to Britain with her destination, London. She bypassed the initial step of applying for her birth certificate, in the hope that the travel agent would solve that problem more quickly. She did have a baptismal certificate, which the agent would use to apply for an official birth certificate.

She made several trips to the travel agent's office in Kingston at a cost she could ill afford. She was frustrated by the delay and solved the problem with an alternative. After waiting several hours in the crowded office for her birth certificate, she heard the name Matilda Mason called several times, without anyone responding. She left the office for a short while, then returned, approached the travel agent and asked, "Have you received the birth certificate for Matilda Mason?"

The agent checked her files and replied, "I called your name over and over and you were not here to answer me. You lucky someone did not steal your identity. Sign this receipt and I will immediately apply for your passport. I see you are going to Birmingham. Are you going to stay with relatives or friends? If you have not made definite arrangements with anyone, I will also find you a place to stay."

"How soon can I get the passport?" Virginia asked.

"It should be ready in three weeks," the agent replied.

Virginia left the island four weeks later, on a ship to her new destination, Birmingham instead of London. No one in her family accompanied her to the pier, nor heard from her since she left. Harry and Tarta had no answers to various questions and speculations about Virginia's whereabout. But they were also surprised that Virginia did not confide in her best friend, Lucy, who inquired every day if Tarta heard from Virginia. "Any word from her yet?" she would ask.

"Not yet," would be Tarta's response.

Despite the secrecy surrounding Virginia's overseas travel, some people speculated that she either went to England, the US, or other countries. Without answers from her family, many of those people speculated that fate was unkind to her. She was either suffering or dead.

Because Tarta had very little experience travelling anywhere, he speculated that Virginia miscalculated the challenges of travelling to an unknown destination so far away in Birmingham and is over-whelmed by difficulties. He spent sleepless nights wondering about various tragedies that befell his granddaughter even before she reached England. First, it's possible that Virginia did not leave the island, because the real Matilda Mason showed up at the pier and pushed Virginia overboard before she could leave the island. Alternatively, Virginia may have started a chain reaction that resulted in Matilda Mason assuming another person's identity, made her getaway to Britain also, where she had a deadly confrontation with Virginia.

At Bulla Shop, the skinniest man in the district whom every-body called Sugar Cane, spoke with certainty about what happened to Virginia. "Mi hear say Virginia gone a foreign with a different name. But mi know say, that woman who Virginia impersonate, work obeah pon Virginia and make duppy turn her inna idiot before she could leave the island. She may be dead by now, but if she is still alive, she turned idiot somewhere on the island and change so much that you wouldn't recognize her."

Bagga Wind countered, "Maybe the duppy was a white man and im wait till Virginia reach England fi throw her overboard. Him finish her up the same way dem finish up Black people who never obey dem rules on slave ships."

Bag-a-Wire whose trademark was a sack of discarded metal scraps, and various claims that he travelled to many parts of the world, had an alternative view. He accepted the possibility that Virginia did reach England. But he said knowingly, "When yu lef ya an go abroad, yu life change. But some people cyaan hangle the change. Dem crack up like glass. Maybe is not duppy that finish off Virginia. She actually crack-up an still ina British mad house."

The fact that Virginia was travelling under an assumed name Matilda Mason, to an unknown destination, reduced the possibilities of government authorities contacting her relatives if she were in trouble. Unlike the arrangements for farmworkers who were contracted to work in the US, Jamaican government did not negotiate agreements with the UK on behalf of Matilda or others travelling to that country. Each person relied on informal support from family members or acquaintances. Some of those acquaintances could have been people she met at the market or the travel agency. They could have given her misleading information. It's also possible that if a mishap occurred, the real Matilda's next of kin, rather than Virginia's family, was notified by the authorities.

There was no funeral for Virginia, because the family was not sure that she died. But her absence was as permanent as death with new resurrections in Harry's mind each day. Each resurrection awakened hopeful new questions, followed by questionable answers. None of which gave Harry a point of contact with his mom.

Harry's unanswered questions included whether his mother's travel plans were based on correct or misleading information. Did she receive the information from a reliable travel agent or from criminal elements she met in Coronation Market? Would previous colleagues in the market have information about her contacts? Did they know her travel destination and specific address? Did they even know her assumed name? He briefly thought Tarta should send her an Abeng signal but rejected the idea because his mother had no conch shells to receive the message. He wondered if ground doves could reveal his mother's whereabouts to Tarta in a dream, but rejected that idea also, because ground doves were tropical birds. They would not survive the cold weather in England and if they did, they would not understand Maroon language.

Harry finally resolved to do everything he possibly could to locate his mother. He would find his mother by hanging about in a place where she had more interesting experiences than those in Plantation Village. He would linger in that place until her spirit and his were tuned in to each other. When that fusion occurred, he would know where she is and be able to end nasty speculations about her whereabouts, with the truth of where her spirit, if not her whole body still lives. But the best thing of all, when their spirits reunite, his orphan status, without both mother and father, would be upgraded. His new status would be more than half of an orphan because of his connection with his mother, the better half of his parents.

CHAPTER 6

Tarta's Surprise

I t was about four o'clock in the evening when Joshua, Barracuda, and Harry left the photographer. They would most likely pass the Market on the way back to the rail yard. But Ras Joshua unexpectedly suggested that they travel to Plantation District to see Tarta and find out if Virginia wrote to the family or anyone in the district. The sudden turn of events surprised Harry. He did not have time to contemplate an explanation to Tarta about why he left home without notifying him or subsequently contacting anyone in the district. He had not rehearsed answers to such questions as "Where did you live? How did you survive? Who are these Rasta men?" People at Bulla Shop would see him before he gets to Tarta's house. What will he say to them? How will they receive him? He felt a mixture of fear and joy, with the joy of seeing Tarta, gaining an edge over fear.

They caught the evening bus at Parade bus stop in Kingston. The name of the bus was Dawn to Dusk Special. Joshua paid for all three of men. The wad of bills he took out of his pocket indicated that he was not going to Plantation District in search of charity. Neither he nor Barracuda had travelled to the parish of St. Thomas before. They applauded the driver's skill at making music with the gearbox as he double clutched when changing to lower gears during the climb of the winding stretch of road called Four Miles Woods.

They enjoyed seeing the Yallahs riverbed, frequently impassible after heavy rains. They saw the stretch of road called White Horses with rushing water falls on the left side of the road and on the right, curling waves with foamy white crest scurrying angrily to the shore. They would cross the Morrant Bay bridge, the longest bridge in the island at that time. They would get to their destination before reaching the Plantain Garden River, the only river in the island that does not flow to the north or to the south.

They got off the bus at about five o'clock in the evening. It was about half an hour before sunset. Joshua and Barracuda got off the bus first. They could feel the stare of many curious eyes. The inquisitive stares at the unknown men were in fact unuttered questions. "Why those men got off the bus at this destination?"

Before the unspoken question was answered, Harry got off the bus. He saw unrecognizable faceless shadows on the ground, of men assembled at Bulla Shop. The fact that their long shadows were less illuminated than they were at noon made it more difficult for Harry to determine who they were. Harry kept looking at the shadows to avoid eye contact as he walked toward the shop. To his surprise, some people quickly recognized him. He was not disguised by his new hairstyle. One person shouted, "Harry! We never believe say you dead."

With the sound of Harry, many people rushed toward him, with total disregard for his accompanying friends. Someone questioned, "Is it true that somebody kidnapped you and work obeah pon you so that you couldn't find your way back home?"

Another shouted instruction to Redman, "Take a shortcut through di gully and don't stop running till you get to Tarta wid di good news dat Harry come back home. Mi can't wait fi si di look pon Tarta face."

Some of Harry's former schoolmates rushed toward him, lifted him in the air, and started singing.

> "Bring back, bring back
> Oh, bring back my Harry to me, to me
> Bring back, bring back
> Oh, bring back my Harry to me."

Tears of joy streamed down Harry's cheeks, because it had been a long time since so many people focused their attention on him. The welcome at Bulla Shop delayed Harry's arrival at Tarta's house by about half an hour. Yet, when he left the shop most of the people who intended to shop, altered their plans to accompany him to the house. They swept his visiting Rasta friends along with the crowd.

Tarta stood at the front of the yard when Harry arrived. So did his mother's best friend Lucy and Elder Adams, who triumphantly exclaimed, "God answers prayers! The prodigal son has returned! Amen."

Harry's heart beating rapidly in his chest, caused him to cough. He began choking on his words, still stuck in his throat. He could barely utter the words, "Good evening, Tarta!" before he and Tarta tightly embraced each other. At the end of the embrace, Harry found his voice and introduced the Rasta strangers to those assembled, "This is Ras Joshua and Ras Barracuda. They are long-time friends of the man everyone here called Mas Victor. I'm sure you remember that he disappeared without a trace before I was born. These men know where Victor is and plan to connect us with each other."

After the introductions, a short get-acquainted session followed between the visitors, Tarta, and Lucy. After the session, Lucy volunteered to rustle up some food for Harry and his visiting friends.

Following the meal, Ras Joshua asked, "Anyone received mail from the post office or heard anything about Virginia?"

After a brief hesitation, Tarta said, "I am too old to start going to the post office and Virginia knowing that, would not waste time writing to me."

Then Lucy hesitantly acknowledged, "I received three letters from Virginia, but never responded, because I did not want to be the one who gave her the bad news that Harry left home without a trace. As a mother myself, I avoided breaking my best friend's heart."

Harry looked over at Ras Joshua and saw that big smile on his face once again. Joshua said to Lucy, "Now that you know that Harry is alive and well, I hope you will respond to Virginia quickly with the good news. But first, can you tell the family how she is doing in England?"

Lucy said, "She left Birmingham where she landed in England. The letter I got four weeks ago said she now has a London address. She mentioned that her Jamaican skills did not prepare her for jobs in England. Fortunately, someone recommended her to a matron in a London hospital and she has been accepted into their nursing program. She lives at the hospital rent-free. She gets food there also. Her current pay is like pocket money, but she knows after she completes the training, she will earn good wages to improve the lives of her family. She always asked me to tell her how Harry and Tarta are doing. I cried when I read her last letter.

"She wrote it on her real birthday, October 30. Not the birth date on her fake travel document. She stated that she did not expect happy birthday wishes from anyone, much less a planned celebration with people, birthday cards, and birthday cake. She did not even have time to reflect on her birthday. She was a first-year nursing student assigned to grub duty on the morning shift of a ward with very sick patients. Additionally, she had to sit an exam in the afternoon. Her primary ward duty was to empty bedpans used during the night by patients, before she made their beds. Although she felt depressed, she did her best to ward off despair, until she remembered that I had not responded to her letters. Even worse she heard no news about her son and her grandfather. She found no consolation in the old saying, 'out of sight out of mind.'

"In an effort to lift her spirit, she offered a helping hand to a middle-aged woman trying to get out of bed. The woman's feet were tangled in the sheet and her upper body was hanging off the bed when she saw Virginia's hand outstretched toward her and yelled loudly, 'Emergency! Emergency! Don't let this monkey woman touch me.' The ward nurse responded immediately. She saw that Virginia's arms were still outstretched toward the woman, but not far enough to rescue the imperiled patient. But the ward nurse immediately reprimanded Virginia for exceeding her responsibilities, 'Look what you have done! I turned my back and you graduate from emptying bedpans to physically assisting patients. At this stage of your career, when you see a patient in distress, your responsibility is to call a qualified nurse, rather than interfering with the patient's care.'

"The ward nurse's insult was an unwelcomed birthday gift that Virginia will never forget. Even worse, Virginia felt that mental effects of the matron's insult would surely shatter her performance on the afternoon's exam. When the shift ended, Virginia went to the dorm and packed her belongings in her board suitcase, in preparation to return to Jamaica. She looked in her purse and realized that she did not have money to pay for her flight home. Tears flowed freely down her cheeks as she contemplated taking the test, failing it and being kicked out of the program anyway. With her back figuratively against the wall, she decided that passing the test would be her birthday gift. She quickly reviewed her class notes before sitting the exam. At the end of the exam, she signed her name Virginia Johnson, instead of her alias, Matilda Mason. The examiner looked at the answer sheets and asked, 'Who is Virginia Johnson?' Matilda stood up, smiled and fearlessly said, 'That's my exam. That signature represents my new identity, my escape from today's humiliating experience inflicted on me by the ward nurse.' Virginia did not include what followed the stunned silence of the examiner and other nursing students."

After Lucy's report, tears of sympathy and joy rolled down Tarta's cheeks as he remarked, "My cup overflows with joy in the presence of Harry and the news about Virginia. It's time we send her encouragement to assure her of our support. Lucy, since you have her address, come by tomorrow and I will tell you the words to put in the letter with a little birthday gift. I'm sure Harry will also want to include a message to her, even if he writes a separate letter later." Lucy agreed to write the letter for Tarta and to give Harry his mother's address. Before returning to her house, she showed Joshua and Barracuda the house Victor lived in. It was currently rented to another tenant, who also became Tarta's friend.

In silence Harry reflected on his intense desire to communicate with his mother and the experience of waiting for her message in Coronation Market, rather than at home. He knew his instincts about her trying to reach him was correct, but he was not in the right place to receive it. He thought about what he would write in the letter. He most certainly would tell her the story of Victor Black's background, where he came from and where he is currently. But even as he thought about Victor's story, he was concerned that including his experience in Coronation Market, which led to the chance encounter with Joshua and Barracuda, could break his mother's heart. He spent a sleepless night thinking about the letter and waiting impatiently for his mother's mailing address.

Harry wrote several drafts in an old school exercise book, before settling on this one.

Plantation District,
Morant Point P.O.

12th June 1959

Dear Mamma,

Hope you are well.

Until last night, I didn't know if you were dead or alive. But I always knew that your spirit would contact me. I thought of various ways by which you would do so, but I never thought you would do it through a letter, because of the risk that your letter would reveal where you are living to immigration police in England.

I hope you know that I wake up every day with you on my mind and you are still there when I go to sleep. Every day I was like a hunting dog trying to sniff out its owner who is hiding behind a new name tag, Matilda Mason. That name is so different from Virginia, that I wonder if you forget who you really are. During my sniffing, I discovered unexpected information about my father. Although everyone called him Mas Victor, his real name is Victor Black. He is from Manchioneal, Portland. His close friends told me that I look just like him. He is from a hard-working Christian family and was ashamed of what he did to make you pregnant. He was so upset that he stowed away to England on a banana boat to escape the bad feelings about what he did to you. I don't know if he got over the bad feelings, when he landed in Portsmouth. I heard that he learned to be an electrician and is working in a factory that makes radios and TVs.

His friends took me to a photographer in Kingston to have my pictures taken last week. This week when they are developed, his friends will send one of my pictures to Victor as a surprise. I will send you one in my next letter. I also plan to visit Victor's parents to learn a little more about him.

God has been good to Tarta. He is still healthy. Everyone, including Lucy, keeps their eyes on him, ready to respond to his needs. But he is very independent. There is not much work on the plantations these days, but he is able to work on the rented plot of land and make a living.

So please don't worry too much about us. Lucy told us you are training to be a nurse. I wonder if it was difficult for you to change from your profession as a higgler to nursing sick white people. Tarta and I will continue praying for your success. I also look forward to that time when our four eyes meet.

Your only son,
Harry

Harry volunteered to mail the letters at Morant Point post office. The familiar three-mile hike to the post office gave him time to adjust to the recent excitement at home. But during the adjustment, he came face-to-face with the reality of his life. He had not finished elementary school as his mom did. He had none of her skills as a higgler. He never spent much time cultivating food crops nor working on the plantations as Tarta did. Even his time at the beach was spent as an observer rather than a fisherman or a sailor. In comparison to the friends he grew up with, he was the only one who travelled to Kingston and gained a limited view of some excitements and difficulties. To the extent that he lived there, the most rewarding experience was his unlikely encounter with two righteous men who sustained him with food, temporary shelter, and friendship. He was in their debt and had no means to repay them.

He also reflected on discussions he overheard by two university students during his sojourn in Coronation Market. One said, "Jamaica has two economic systems. At the top is the capitalist system, a canopy with ties to international markets and money, because of the items it produced. Below that canopy, the local economy is exemplified by Coronation Market activities. People at the top, reign supreme over property and labor, in their single-minded pursuit of making profit and becoming richer. People below the canopy have very little resources to sustain their daily living. They are poorly paid by canopy employers. But when they are self-employed below the canopy in Coronation Market activities, their incomes are barely enough to keep pace with their cost of living. The two systems were not designed to operate as co-equals. The dominant capitalist system marginalized the other system."

The more Harry reflected on the two economic systems, the more convinced he became that a few people in the economic canopy, confined most Jamaicans to ground level economic activities, exemplified by direct exchanges between individuals in Coronation Market systems. Unfortunately, near-sighted people at ground level who fail to see the big economic picture, do no more for themselves than sleep walking in the Market. They are always exposed to the consequences of decisions from above, but not the other way around. Some Black people who were conscious of the economic injustice that made rich people richer and poor people poorer, cry out, "Change the system! Back to Africa." But Harry did not hear practical ideas that would make desirable improvements in Jamaica or in the motherland of Africa.

After Harry returned home, he had a desire to discuss the subject of Coronation Market with Tarta, Lucy, Joshua, and Barracuda. Rather than focusing on his experience in the Market, he would share the story about the capitalist and market systems and why most Jamaicans barely earn enough to buy food and little else. But Tarta started the conversation by asking Harry, "Why did you decide to become a Rasta man like your father?" The question did not make Harry feel that Tarta was accusing him of doing something wrong. Instead, Harry felt that Tarta was trying to learn about the new religion. But he also felt he did not know enough about the Rata doctrine to explain it to Tarta. Nor did he feel like he was a Rasta, even though his hairstyle suggested that he was. So, he asked his friends to explain their beliefs to Tarta.

"Ras Joshua and Barracuda, you know more about Rasta doctrines than I will ever learn. Please tell Tarta why you choose to be Rasta men," said Harry.

Ras Joshua responded, "Tarta, you did a wonderful job training Harry about Black people that's worth remembering. He not only remembered, but shared the stories about Nanny, Paul Bogle, and the Maroons who never lost the African spirit to fight oppression. In today's Jamaica, white people and puppet Black people misinterpret the Bible to hide the truth and continue the oppression. Black people were the original Israelites. White people were Babylonians who stole our people from the home of their ancestors in Africa. There is an urgent need for Black people to break the white man's spell that keep us in bondage and from returning to Africa. It's important to note this fact. In 1930, a black man, Haile Selassie, who lived in the African country of Ethiopia, was crowned King of Kings, Lord of Lords. His coronation was the fulfillment of biblical prophecy. Since then, Black people know that the living God is a Black man in Africa, not the spirit of some white man living above the clouds. Give me your Bible and I will read two passages to prove that God was both Ethiopian and black."

> *Glorious things are spoken of thee O City of God. Selah*
> *I will make mention of Rehab and Babylon to them that*
> *know me: behold Philistia, and Tyre, with Ethiopia;*
> *this man was born there. (Psalm 87:3-4)*

> *For the hurt of the daughter of my people I hurt; I am*
> *black; astonishment has taken hold of me. (Jeremiah 8:21)*

"These are not my words. The Bible just declared that God was born in Ethiopia and the prophet Jeremiah was astonished that he was black. These are prophetic words in the Bible that is being fulfilled in our time. Here is another truth about Rasta. We are a nonviolent people. That's partly why we eat the fruits and herbs of the field instead of killing animals for our food. And speaking of herbs, we smoke the same herb smoked by King Solomon, the wisest man that ever lived hundreds of years ago. After his death, his followers grew the weed on his tomb. That's the herb people now call ganja. We smoke it just like the wisest man did. Here in Babylon, the authorities condemn us for continuing to enlighten ourselves with the use of the weed. Babylon cannot prevail against the I and I!"

Tarta thanked Joshua for his explanation and for extending his hand of friendship to his great-grandson and for the Bible lesson. "Harry is my only great-grandchild. He is my most precious possession, now that I have lost my wife, his grandmother, and not sure when or if I will ever see his mother again. Regarding your Bible lesson, I never heard anyone interpret the Bible the way you did. Was your wisdom gained from smoking ganga?" Everyone laughed, but Joshua, with an unusual sense of humility, did not answer the question.

Now that preliminaries of the religion were out of the way, Harry was hungry for more knowledge about wisdom and wealth. He started with a story of Solomon that he remembered from Sunday school. "I remember hearing two things about King Solomon in Sunday school. He was the wisest and the richest man living at that time. Do you know how he became so rich? I'll tell you. One night he had a dream that he was in a difficult situation with the people around him and he asked God for wisdom to distinguish between good and evil. God was very pleased that Solomon asked for wisdom rather than wealth or long life. So, God reward Solomon's unselfish request by giving him wisdom without any hesitation. But God also gave Solomon something else that he never asked for. That thing was wealth. He woke up from that dream, blessed with both wisdom, meaning good judgement and with wealth. With those blessings, Solomon reached the top of his nation and the surrounding nations.

He was not at the bottom. He had free reign over the creation of wealth for himself and his people. He was not a slave in a foreign land. We here in Jamaica and Black people all over the world are not like Solomon. We are more like the Jamaican turkey vulture we call John Crow. We scavenge at the bottom of society for our existence. We are in a big Coronation Market, with nothing to sell and no money to buy necessities. I remember Ras Joshua telling me that people who had nothing to sell nor money to buy in Coronation Market were in the wrong place. Where is our place? Can we rise to the top like King Solomon, if we don't make wisdom our priority? How does smoking the weed contribute to practical wisdom of knowing the difference between good and evil?"

Barracuda cleared his throat in preparation to answer Harry's questions. "It is true that King Solomon had a head start with wisdom, followed by riches. It is also true that he was not a slave. He had the freedom to carry out the plan that God ordained for him. We are not that lucky. We must start by breaking the chains of enslavement in every form that we encounter it, no matter if the slave master is black or white. Remember now. Black people sold us into slavery. White people bought us. Which of the two do you prefer?"

He paused, but there was no response, so he continued by quoting a Bible verse from James 3:17, "But the wisdom from above is first pure, then peaceable, gentle, and easy to be entreated, full of mercy and good fruits, without partiality, and without hypocrisy. Think about the wonderful world we would be living in if we had that kind of wisdom before we got rich. We would not be hypocrites like Nanny who won a battle against white people in the eastern parish of Portland and then joined them in a conspiracy against Cudjo, a fellow Maroon, who was fighting for a just cause in the western parish of Trelawny. We would not have betrayed Paul Bogle to white people who hanged him for trying to seek improvement in wages of poor Black people. Placing wisdom ahead of riches is like harnessing a horse to haul a cart full of goods that benefit everyone. No one gets rich at another person's expense. But getting riches before being wise enough to know good from evil is putting the cart before the horse.

Yes, the I and I said, wisdom is required to know our enemies and the various ways by which we are chained to their wickedness. He also said it is wise to learn some of the white man's tricks of unlocking the hidden treasures beneath the earth, on the land, in the seas, and in the air above the earth."

By the look on everyone's face, it was obvious that Barracuda said something that made sense. But for Harry who experienced his kindness in Kingston, his actions spoke even louder than his voice. He bought Harry clothes, he befriended him, he helped him discover his father's roots in Portland. Unlike a hypocrite, he practiced what he preached. Harry felt grateful for Barracuda's explanation of the rightful place of wisdom in everyone's life and quietly agreed that the world would be a better place if wisdom, rather than riches, were the priority.

After the getting to-know-you discussion opened them up to one another, everyone seemed more relaxed, although the newcomers to the district shouldered the bigger burden of making themselves known to their host. Forehead furrows above frown lines receded. Glints of joy sparkled in eyes that a few minutes earlier were quizzical, uncertain or even suspicious. Lips easily parted to reveal genuine smiles. Although Harry wanted to be lighthearted, he couldn't help thinking about what will happen next. When will his newly found friends return to Kingston? Will they expect him to return with them? Will they accompany him to Portland to meet his father's parents before returning to Kingston? When will he get the pictures he promised to send to his mother?

Before any of the questions could be answered, Tarta suggested that Harry take the men on a walking tour of the district. Fortunately, the men were curious to explore the district where their friend Victor used to live. The tour started at about ten o'clock in the morning. It was a sunny summer day and nature was cooperating fully. The sun rose about four hours earlier. It was near the halfway mark in the sky, as it moved from sunrise in the east to sunset in the west. Its rays streamed through thin layers of white clouds merrily floating across the sky like puffs of windblown smoke. A gentle breeze filled with moisture from the sea kept them cool.

Unlike the perpetual jarring noises of shunting trains, automobile traffic, and higglers peddling various goods in Kingston, the men heard more soothing sounds in the less densely populated Plantation Village. They heard playful sounds of children, leaves flopping in the wind, and various bird songs. There were high pitch songs by small birds called ants quits. There were screeching sounds of chicken hawks flying overhead in search of food, the cooing sounds of barble doves and the drilling sounds of the woodpecker. They even heard children mimicking the nightingales' song with the words, "You si mi foot? You si mi foot? No laugh, no laugh. Sickness! Sickness!" Those sounds followed the men everywhere they went in the district.

There were no paved roads in the district. In fact, the roads were not intentionally designed by land surveyors. They were convenient paths either carved out by rainwater or repeatedly trampled by people or their domestic animals. There were no street addresses. Places were identified by special shade trees or other recognizable landmarks. The district had two main sections. The valley nearer to the river was called Bottom Land. There, people got drinking water and washed their clothes. The higher ground nearer to the main road was called Top Land. The tour started at Bottom Land where Tarta lived. The thatched houses on either side of the foot path were shielded from view by a variety of hedges. On the right were a mixture of croton shrubs with a purple bias and hibiscus shrubs with a wider variety of colors raging from lily white to dark red. It was obvious from the activities of humming birds, butterflies, bees, and other insects that the hibiscus blossoms provided more tempting treats. The rival hedges on the other side of the path included bougainvillea plants with purple, gold, and white flowers.

The foot path abruptly ended at a complex of four houses called Balm Yard. It was a place where four sisters and their families used herbal remedies and the spiritual practice of obeah to drive out evil spirits and heal their victims. Sister Angel, the youngest sister, warmly welcomed Harry and his visiting friends. She gave them a quick tour of the yard with its variety of fruit trees and a playing field for the children. The ground was swept clean of litter, except for the purple blossoms covering the ground under the Otaheite apple trees.

After Balm Yard, Harry showed his friends an alternative path to both the river and Top Land. It was to the right of Balm Yard under the cover of lush guava trees that acquired the name Guava Walk. Both paths from Balm Yard and Guava Walk merged under a very large cotton tree, where people sought protection from direct heat of the sun. They saw people conversing under shade tree, some with laundry baskets, others with buckets of water on their heads.

The road from Cotton Tree to Top Land was steep, but wider than the path from Bottom Land. It was covered with pebble stones. It passed Bulla Shop and went west to the part of the district where most residents lived. The hedges along the path were not as spectacular as those at Bottom Land, nor as protective of the people living in the yards. Harry and his friends could see people engaged in a variety of yard work. They were sweeping up thrash, chopping firewood, washing clothes in small wash pans, and having lively conversations. Toward the end of the path, houses on the left side of the path gave way to the beginning of a huge cow pasture with many cows grazing on the grass. Harry told the men stories about him and his youthful friends playing in the pasture, while being afraid of possible attack by unpredictably disgruntled bulls. They completed the tour in about two hours and returned to Tarta's house for refreshment, which included ice cold lemonade.

After three days in Plantation District, Harry's Rasta friends decided to return to Kingston. Harry also agreed to join them, partly because he needed their support to get the pictures from the photographer that he planned to send to his mother. He embraced Tarta. Tears freely flowing down both their cheeks, while Tarta said his parting words, "The last time you left here my hair was black. The next day people could hardly recognize me, because my hair turned white overnight. I had no idea where you went, what danger you were in, what I said or did to make you walk away from our home, our relationship, and storytelling times about our Maroon ancestors. I was left with wild imaginations, but could give no satisfactory answer about you to the living or the dead. To the living I said, 'Him gone,' but Mammy was not satisfied with that answer and kept invading my dreams each night for updates. In her frustration she said, 'I was supposed to be resting in peace, but how can I, when our children are driftwood in an endless angry ocean?' Mammy and I seldom quarreled when she was alive, but in my dream disputes, I push back against her accusations. I would say to her, 'You are the ghost that we released to dwell with the ancestors and share the responsibility of protecting our family. What have you done? Why aren't you giving me information about Virginia and Harry, rather than asking me questions about them? You should know that I don't have a clue where they are.' But when I awake from the conflict with Mammy, I was still suffering from real hopelessness, because you and everyone dear to me were gone, and I had nothing to live for. Now, unlike then, I am confident that God will continue to protect you when we are apart. Walk good my boy and may your Maroon light brighten the path of others."

As Harry and his friends departed, Harry said to Tarta, "This is not a goodbye, because my absence will always be temporary."

With those words from Harry, Tarta showed no concern that Harry would disappear again. He even extended return invitation to Harry's friends. Following the goodbyes, Harry and his friends left on the evening bus to Kingston.

The trip back to Kingston was uneventful, and the shack they lived in at the rail yard was still standing. Several notes tucked under the entrance to the shack confirmed that people had visited the shack and needed responses from Joshua and Barracuda. Harry later learned that the messages were more related to proposed meeting schedules and their ganja business, rather than concerns about their personal well-being. Despite what seemed like urgent messages, the men gave priority to visiting the photographer the next day.

When they arrived, Harry was surprised to see an enlarged portrait of himself displayed on a wall in the photo studio. It was the first time he saw what he looked like to other people. He had never seen himself in a mirror. There wasn't a mirror at Tarta's house where he grew up nor at the shack in Kingston where he most recently resided with the brethren. The only likeness of himself that he saw previously, was shimmering out of focus reflections in river water. Unlike those reflections, the studio photographs made him look like people in books and magazines. He loved the pictures of himself and readily consented to Snapper's proposal to display one portrait inside the studio and one outside the entrance to attract new customers interested in having their pictures taken. After he consented to that deal, Snapper said, "I heard that this is the first time you see a pretty picture of yourself, so I'm going to give you a few of them for keepsake and to share with your family. Secondly, I'll give you one as large as those in the studio, but you will have to select the one you like best. Finally, because I believe you will bring me good luck, I won't charge you for any of the pictures."

When Harry and his friends left Snapper's studio, they were beaming with happiness. They also anticipated similar reaction from Victor when he receives Harry's letter with pictures of his well-known friends and his unknown son.

After they returned to the shack, Harry's friends left him to follow up on their messages. During their absence, Harry admired the pictures and wrote rough draft of the letter he would send with a few photos to his mother. Later, Harry and his friends talked about their uplifting experience in Plantation District. Some highlights included tranquility that sharply contrasted the jarring noises of the train yard; basking in the delicate light of Tarta's curiosity and hospitality; the stimulating reasoning sessions, especially those about the wisdom needed to unlock the storehouse of God's riches, even the riches of Zion.

Joshua acknowledged his responsibility to tell people the truth about Jah and to demonstrate how wise people should live with one another. He also acknowledged that living in the train yard did not achieve those two objectives. Partly because the living arrangement was not a symbol of good living, but downright failure or extreme lack of vanity, comparable to what people in olden times use to do when they cover themselves with sackcloth and ashes. But after the Plantation District visit, he is more inclined to share the feelings King David expressed in Psalm 29 when he said, "Thou hast put off my sackcloth and girded me with gladness."

In that refreshed mood, Joshua expressed the following idea. "Babylon was a place of exile and as it was in the beginning, so it is even now. Most people in exile strive to return to the places from which they were stolen. This modern Babylon is not simply a physical location, it is also a state of mind that obscures the realities of Zion. Babylon is everywhere the Black man is enslaved physically and mentally and lives in subjugation to other people. It could be in Jamaica, England, America, or Africa. So, the simple act of physically moving from one country to another in the hope of finding people who will give him freedom and treat him as a fellow human, will not guarantee his freedom. First, he must develop freedom strategies in the places of enslavement and replicate those strategies, with necessary modifications in every place he is forced or choose to live."

He continued by emphasizing that the Bible makes it clear that Zion is the opposite of Babylon. Its symbolic importance relates to the state of mind in which people's reliance on Jah and acknowledgement of His protection, builds their confidence into a psychologically unmovable mountain. He then stood up to emphasize this idea. "We don't have to move! Here me now. We don't have to move from Jamaica. In fact, the good book, in Psalm 125:1-2 said, 'They that wait upon the Lord, shall be like Mount Zion, which cannot be moved, but abideth forever. As the mountains are round about Jerusalem, so the Lord is round about his people from henceforth even forever.'"

Joshua concluded his reflections by saying, "Brethren, we no have fi lef Jamaica if the Lord is round about us. Further, we no have fi live in a shack at train yard. If we remember fi put di wisdom horse in front of our money cart, rather than putting greed and selfishness in front, Jah will bless us with riches, like him bless Solomon. Yes, brethren, when we become wise, we can find riches right here, in Jamaica, and that's what me ago do."

CHAPTER 7

Harry's Extended Family

U nlike Joshua, Barracuda did not articulate his opinion about finding wisdom and riches in Jamaica, he acted immediately on another decision. The next morning, he invited Harry to join him on a visit to Victor's parents in Manchioneal. They boarded the 10:00 AM bus at Parade, which travelled the longer route from Kingston, through the parishes of St. Andrews and St. Mary. The bus travelling the shorter route through St. Thomas would not leave Parade until 4:00 PM, and when they arrived at their destination, their surprise visit would be too late at night. Harry looked forward to the new experience of driving through the hair pin turns of the spiral mountain path called Junction. From his window seat on the bus, he could see the deep ravines on either side of the road. He was often scared when the bus listed on one side and then the other while the chauffer negotiated tight corners up and down the mountain. But passengers who were accustomed to traveling that route often cheered spontaneously at the sounds of the driver deftly shifting gears to control the treacherous climb and descent of the bus.

The churning in Harry's stomach decreased after the bus passed through the parish of St. Mary and reached the less treacherous area of Hope Bay in Portland. In that more relaxed mode, he enjoyed the scenery of alternating green vegetation and the blue waters of the sea along the remaining way to Manchioneal. The road was designed to follow the beautiful coastline which revealed inviting glimpses of coves, lagoons, and sandy beaches. The highway scenery prepared Harry for a positive experience when he reached his grandparents' home.

He and Barracuda arrived at a yard enclosed by shrubbery and a swinging wooden gate. In front of the partially opened gate two men were in conversation. Barracuda's greetings interrupted the conversation. "Good evening, Mr. Amos and Mas Neh."

In response, Mr. Amos said, "Fan mi wid a brick! Is that you, David? How come you make the northeast wind blow you back to Portland?"

That was the first time Harry heard Barracuda answer to the name David. "Yes, sir, it's me. I'm here on a surprise visit, which might as well begin with you. Please look at this young man and tell me who you see."

Mr. Amos said, "If him wasn't so young I would mistake him for Victor."

"That's the same way I felt when I saw him in Kingston. His name is Harry. Here is the surprise. He is Victor's son, and I am here to introduce him to you, Miss Ruth, and the rest of the family," said David with satisfied grin on his face.

Harry's grandfather was about fifty-five years old, but his body looked more like a thirty-year-old weightlifter. If he were surprised to hear that Harry was Victor's son, he didn't show it. He invited them into the yard to meet the other family member. As they walked to the house, Mr. Amos asked David if he maintained his friendship with Victor. David responded that they were not in regular contact, but Victor's last letter stated that he was an electrician in London.

The walkway to the house was long. It was paved with smooth pebbles collected from the beach. There were a variety of potted ferns on either side of the walk way. Unlike the houses in Plantation District, this house was made with bricks and seemed more durable. It was much larger than Tarta's house, but not as large as backra people house on the plantations in St. Thomas.

"Ruth, we have company!" That's how Harry's grandfather announced their arrival at the entrance to the house. The grandmother had a curious look on her face when she opened the door. She did not recognize David who was standing behind Mr. Amos, while deliberately blocking Harry from her full view. She responded playfully by saying, "Dadda, you say we have company, no need fi play hide and seek with me." She then peered over Dadda's shoulders and was surprised when she saw that David had changed into a Rasta man.

"Boy, when did you turn Rasta? But Mi glad fi si you just the same. We miss having you and Victor around us. Both of you were wonderful young men when you left home in search of new experience in Kingston. Who is the young man behind you?" Before David responded, Mr. Amos and Ms. Ruth engaged in playful question and answer game.

"Ruth, guess who this young man is."

"You always playing games with me. I know I have never seen this young man before, so how could I guess who he is?"

"Are you sure you have never seen him?"

"I'm sure he doesn't live in the district, so where would I have seen him? What's your name, young man?"

"My name is Harry, ma'am. I'm Victor's son."

"Good God Almighty! You certainly have Victor's face. Come give your grandmother a big hug. Where have you been that I never heard about you? David and your father were best friends when they lived in this district. I am glad he brought you to us."

After that greeting, she welcomed them into the house and served cold glasses of sweetened lemonade while she reheated a meal for her guests. When David informed her that he no longer ate meat, she quickly picked chou-chou, callaloo, and susumber from her garden and made vegetable stew for him. He and Harry had a hearty meal which included yellow yam, green bananas, and flower dumplings. Harry was served curry goat in addition to some of the vegetable stew.

During the meal, Harry told his new grandparents his background in Plantation District, including stories about Tarta and his mother who was currently studying nursing in England. He also talked about his mother's plight, after Victor took advantage of her as a teenage girl, then abandon her and her child. He added that he never met Victor. He did not tell them how he met David, nor that in Kingston, David was called Barracuda. But he expressed gratitude to David for telling him amusing stories about young Victor, when both were growing up in Portland. He also shared that David invited him on the visit to meet them in their Portland home in the hope that they would accept him as their grandchild. He ended his background story by offering his grandparents the recent photo of himself as keepsake.

Harry's grandmother smiled broadly as she took the picture from him and walked to the dressing table in the living room. She quickly decided to place it between the framed pictures of her wedding and a picture of King George V1 of England. Her picture was to the left and the King's picture was to the right. There were no other pictures in that room. There was no picture of Victor, nor his brothers and sisters, that could confirm Harry's resemblance to the family. At the end of what seemed like a ceremonial welcome, she invited her husband to look at how she displayed the picture. His approving smile seemed to confirm their acceptance of Harry as a family member.

David broke his silence by recounting stories of his and Victor's voyages of discovery. "Unlike Columbus, we did not have a compass, not even one to misguide us, as it did the great discoverer, who lost his way to India and accidentally landed in the West Indies instead. We arrived in Kingston as simple country boys unprepared to deal with the widespread selfishness of people we encountered. People were fighting for themselves and did not mind hurting others to get what they wanted. It was a dog eat dog world, where everything was up for grab. It was as though the higgler spirit of Coronation Market had spread all over Kingston. Everything had a price. But people who had nothing to sell and no money to buy became invisible among the garbage that they scavenged for unwanted food during the day and where they slept uncomfortably during the night. They eventually dropped to the bottom of the society and became victims of that harsh reality.

"We survived the best way we could, while listening to many people's arguments about various forms of oppression. We agreed with what we heard in the Rasta doctrine that God had a special relationship with Black people. We accepted that doctrine and refused to be an undesirable commodity of useless exchange in any type of Coronation Market. We also decided to use that knowledge to break our mental chains of slavery in Jamaica and return to the motherland of Africa. But over time as our *overstanding* matured, the Fada revealed to us, that the Almighty is everywhere and so are his riches. Therefore, the most important thing we need is the wisdom of how to harvest God's riches. See, Victor gained the wisdom of an electrician and will harvest the riches associated with that trade in England or anywhere in the world he decides to live. Look at Harry's mother, she will harvest the riches of the nursing trade anywhere in the world, after she finish her training in England. Finally, look at you and Mr. Amos, both of you are harvesting God's riches right here in Portland. Will you ever be as rich as the white backra man? Maybe not. But more important, you are not his slave.

"The Fada also taught me during my sojourn in Kingston that the archenemies of righteousness are selfishness and greed. The selfish person is stuck in the devil's trap of always taking and never giving. His twin brother's greed always wants more without ever being satisfied. Together they store up riches while losing basic humanity in the devil's trap of wickedness. Jah expects me to share the blessings I receive from Him with others that are less fortunate. So, at this point in my life, I'm pursuing wisdom, in anticipation of the riches Jah wants me to share with His needy children. It is in that spirit that I brought Harry to meet you. While my gift of bringing you and Harry together is not money, I believe it is an experience that will make both your lives richer. As dem say in the white man's Bible, 'such as I have, give I thee.' In my next letter to Victor I will report my joyful reunion with you and your warm reception of Harry."

By the next morning news of David's return to the village had spread through the district to Victor's brothers and sister. Ina arrived first, followed shortly by Nathaniel and Winston. They seemed surprised that both David and Harry wore dreadlocks like Rasta men. But lingering friendship with David prevented them from expressing negative feelings about Rasta. They greeted Harry and welcomed him to the family, then quickly turned to David with questions about life in Kingston. They reportedly visited the capital city a few times but did not stay long enough to know the place well.

David told them, "If you asked one hundred people about Kingston, you could get one hundred different answers related to the part of Kingston each person knew best. There is the upscale Kings Street section with big savings and commercial banks, government offices, and fancy shops owned by rich Syrian people, stocked with jewelry and other expensive merchandise. It's usually the first place tourists see when they got off luxury ships in Kingston Harbor. There is the area called Parade to the north of Kings Street. It's a beehive of activities. There, desk job people wearing white shirts and ties, rub shoulders against working class people with and without shirts. They shuffle their way through various size crowds or streams of other people flowing in many directions to surrounding handcarts with snacks such as beef patties; roasted peanuts; ice-cold raw oysters; a variety of cold drinks, including Irish Moss made from seaweed; cut cakes; and greater cakes made from coconuts. Between parade and Coronation Market to the west, there is a Kingston filled with street vendors, some hawking cheap versions of items reportedly sold on Kings Street. It is also a place where naïve visitors and even less vigilant residents become victims of scam artists and pickpockets, such as one-arm Man-Rat. He operated at nights and was clever enough to steal shoes off people's feet. For instance, one Christmas eve night at Parade, he attempted to steal a woman's shoes while her feet were dangling under the park bench. After his first attempt, she wiggled her left foot back into her shoe, without any thought of what was happening. During his second attempt, she jokingly told her boyfriend sitting beside her, that a duppy under the bench was trying to steal her shoes. Although her friend was afraid of the evil spirits called duppy, he bravely looked under the bench to verify the mystery. To his surprise, he came face-to-face, not with a ghost, but the culprit Man-Rat. Both men scuffled briefly under the bench, but the boyfriend was no match for Man-Rat's agility. The one-arm bandit emerged with the shoe and might have gotten away with it, if he had not dropped the shoe when he lost his balance and stumbled over various stalls. The boyfriend recovered the shoe. But many vendors who had valuable ceramics on their stalls for sale, lost everything when Man-Rat forced his way through their stalls like a bulldozer."

David concluded his Kingston story, by describing where he lives. "I live in the industrial part of west Kingston, near the rail yard and the factories. It is easily the noisiest part of town. It is a place where newcomers to the city live in hope or died in despair. Or as some Kingstonians who played with words would say in contrasting upscale Hope Gardens with working class Constant Spring, 'live in Hope or die in Constant Spring.'"

At the end of their discussion, David told them he was going to visit his parents who lived a half a mile away. He gave Harry the option of going along with him or continuing the visit with his grandparents. Harry chose to accompany David, to witness the family reunion. They said goodbye to Harry's relatives and promised a return visit, without specifying a time.

Rather than walking along the main road to his parents' house, David led Harry along the unpaved back roads where most people in the district lived. Their walking was punctuated by brief greetings of some neighbors and respectful hellos to others along the way. When they reached his parents' house, his arrival was announced by the excited welcome of a barking dog that had not forgotten David. The dog was jet black, with white markings under its eyes, on its feet, and the tip of its tail. He barked, he ran toward David, sniffed him, licked his hands, ran around him in circles, ran toward the house, picked up a twig in its mouth and brought it to David. They then engaged in a game they used to play many years ago. David took the twig from the dog's mouth, threw it toward the house, and joyfully watched as the dog raced to catch it. The dog was unconcerned about Harry as a threat to the family, while its attention was focused on David.

The dog's playful barking made the family aware that they had a friendly visitor. David's mother was the first family member to see him. She barely recognized him with his dreadlocks and beard, but his relationship with the dog was unmistakable. He walked toward the door that his mother opened wider as he approached her. They embraced. Tears of joy flowed freely down her cheeks. David was the first to speak.

"Good morning, Mamma! You look like you have been taking care of yourself. How is Daddy, Joyce, and Amos?"

"Everybody is doing well. We often wonder about you. Where in Kingston you lived. Sometimes we thought the worse, that your life was so hard, or that you got in trouble with the law why we didn't hear from you. But we never stop praying that Masa God will have mercy pon you."

David's mother was about five feet six inches tall. Her hair, with black and gray strands, was combed into three plaits. One on each side of her head and one at the back. Beads of sweat accumulated on her brow, then slowly mingled with the tears flowing down her cheeks. The arms with which she embraced David seemed physically strong but gentle. The length of her floral dress with a blue background extended to her knees. The uneven stitches in the hem, left little doubt that the dress was made locally, most likely handsewn, possibly by her.

When her eyes met Harry's, she broke her embrace of David to ask, "Who is the young man travelling with you?"

"He is Victor's son. His name is Harry. He grew up in the adjoining parish of St. Thomas. Both his parents are now living in England, so when I discovered that he was Victor's son, I brought him to meet his father's parents and other relatives."

While shaking Harry's hand she said, "Welcome to Portland. I am glad to meet you and to know that you have made a connection with your family in this parish."

Harry replied, "I am also glad to meet you, Miss Mamma. But I'm even more glad to witness the family reunion between you and David."

On the way to the house, Harry walked behind David and his mother. The dog following behind him. But when he looked over his shoulder the dog was not walking. He prostrated himself on the grass adjoining the path, his front legs pulling him forward with the support of his outstretched hind legs. It was another display of the dog's happiness. Harry tapped David's shoulder and pointed to the dog crawling behind. David looked and wiped tears from his eyes as he was overcome by the emotional reaction to his dog's welcome and his mother's loving embrace. At that moment, it seemed unlikely that he could walk away from that loving experience and return to the harsh realities of a hut in Kingston rail yard.

The house was smaller than Mr. Amos's house, but it was like the surrounding houses, a sturdy three-bedroom house with wooden sidings and zinc roof. All the houses were noticeably sturdier than those in Plantation District. David and Harry stopped in the shade of a huge number-eleven mango tree, while David's mother took their travel bags into the house.

While she was preparing lemonade for them, David's father, Mr. Jones, arrived from work earlier than expected. He heard the good news that his son was in the village. He saw David and Harry sitting under the tree and greeted them. "Hello, David, you look different from how you used to look when you were living here. I am proud of you for bringing Victor's son to meet his grandparents. That act of kindness tells me that regardless of what you look like now, your heart is in the right place. It is written in the Bible, 'Train a child in the way he should go and when he is old he will never depart from it.'"

"Good afternoon, Dadda! I know my unexpected visit is a big surprise to you and Mamma. Thank you for the warm welcome. I know you have many questions about what I have been doing in Kingston since I left home. But I believe you will be in a better frame of mind to hear what I have to say, after you have eaten dinner and relax."

The after-dinner conversation continued with Mr. Jones' answers to David's questions about David's siblings, Joyce and Amos. "Just like you, your sister and brother outgrew Portland. Amos became a merchant seaman and drops in to see us sometimes when the ship docks in Port Antonio. He got the job on the ship a few years after he was working at the wharf in Port Antonio. Being a jocular fellow, he made friends with some of the white men working on banana boats. Before long, he was even talking to a captain. To make a long story short, the captain offered him a job as a steward assistant on a British merchant ship.

"He said he works closely with the chief steward to stock food and cleaning supplies in the storerooms. He assists in preparing and serving meals as well as with the cleaning jobs. The working hours are long, and the work is challenging especially when there is turbulence due to bad weather conditions. But there is a bright side. He has travelled all over the world and got a glimpse of how many other people live in other countries. He saw rich people and poor people everywhere, even in places where people are of the same skin color. He compared countries to ships in the ocean. They need captains to guide, control, and prevent them from running aground. Good captains also provide adequate supplies and keep the crew happy, while getting them to do their jobs. Based on his experience at sea, he feels that Jamaica has two basic problems. First, it has inexperienced captains whose limited navigation skills could result in the ship of state running aground. Second, their captains fail to distribute adequate supplies for maintenance of the government and satisfying people's needs. He was not surprised that many people like himself have jumped ship from the island and he wouldn't be surprise if many more will follow.

"The first time he told me about the job, I pictured him as a drunken sailor. The ones we see in Port Antonio, stumbling around with a prostitute as a guide. I worried that I could not protect him and that in his drunkenness he couldn't even hear the still small voice of God. But every time I have seen and heard from him since he got that job, he was sober. He seems to be successfully navigating his way around the ship and the world. He is learning to cook like a chef and proudly show off his skills in our kitchen. He wants to be the first Jamaican chief steward on a ship. He even believes he could liven up the food with Portland style jerk pork, curry chicken, and escovitche fish.

"Joyce is also overseas. She works as a nanny for a rich white family in Halifax, Nova Scotia. I give you one chance to guess how she got that job."

David hesitated to speak, while he reviewed various possibilities in his mind. He could not think of any family contacts in Canada. Although Amos was overseas, he was stationed in England, and even if he were in Canada, it's unlikely that he would know any rich family. His sister did not work in Jamaican tourist resorts, where she would have met people from Canada. He was still thinking when his father said, "Time's up! You take too long to guess the answer. If you were thinking that Amos made the contact but had doubts about that answer, you would have been right. Yes, thanks to your brother, Amos, your sister got a job in Canada. On one of his voyages he met sailors from Nova Scotia who were bragging about the beautiful Halifax harbor and its fishing activities. Their description of summertime activities reminded him of Port Antonio. It also occurred to him that his sister would enjoy visiting that place, at least during the summer. He asked the sailors to contact him if they ever heard that anyone in Halifax was looking for domestic help. Not long afterward a sailor told him that the harbormaster's wife, Mrs. O'Conner, needed a nanny to help her with the children. Your sister has been gone a year now and her letters make us feel that she is getting along well with her employer. She said they may be visiting Jamaica soon.

"That's our story. What do you have to say for yourself?"

Up to this time in Harry's experience with David/Barracuda, he heard very little about David's relationship with his father. He heard of his relationship with Victor in Portland before they went to Kingston. He knew of David's relationship with Ras Joshua in Kingston, after Victor relocated to St. Thomas. So, he was curious to hear what David was going say. He sat with full attention to listen to the story David would tell his parents about conversion to a Rasta man.

He started by saying, "My early experience in Kingston was like taking purgative or what country people called wash out. Do you remember the homemade medicines you and mamma use to give us children at the end of a summer feast of fruits, including guava, guineps, jackfruit, mammee, mangoes, and soursop to wash out our system before we returned to school? Even though country belly-running experiences were bad, those I experienced in the early days in Kingston were worse. Yes, the experience in Kingston was more intense. It included recurring mental and physical sensation of needing to shit, but without the sensation of being able to finish shitting. The experience was made worse by the fact that there was nothing like old newspaper or green tree leaves to wipe my behind, if or when I stop shitting. Did I say the experience was bad? Let me rephrase. It was rotten! It stunk!"

He continued, "Aunt Ruby's house was the first place I lived when I moved to Kingston. People said she owned the house, although she never admitted that to me. She admitted owning a sidewalk stall in front of the house. It was stocked with produce she purchased at Coronation Market to resell to people who were willing to pay a little more for items from the market, if someone would save them the trouble of going to the Market. Her day started shortly after midnight. That allowed enough time for her to walk a mile and a half to the market before it opened at one o'clock in the morning. She did this activity three times a week. She had very little time to do anything else but go to the Market and sell the produce. She seemed to be a good businesswoman. She charged more than she paid for the products at the Market, but not too much to discourage her customers from continuing to buy produce from her. She also sold other items that attracted people to her stall. They included fruits and snacks, especially those that mothers would buy for their children. A favorite was snow cones, which was shaved ice covered with various colored fruit syrups. Sometimes it seemed to me that some parents were lured to the stall by the snow cones for the children, but while there, changed their minds to buy additional items such as yams, sweet potatoes, pumpkins, gungo peas, and seasoning to make soup for dinner.

"As a condition for living in her house, she expected me to wake up and go with her to the Market. But waking up before midnight three times a week was difficult for me. I had to go to bed early, even though I was not sleepy. I would leave the house with her before dawn even if I had not slept earlier. I had very little time to sleep night or day. Secondly, she did not think it was necessary to pay me, because my services were regarded as boarding fee. After a while, I decided to leave her place and strike out on my own."

Mamma interrupted David with her comment. "So, you were working like her donkey? She loaded you down with bags of food she bought in the market and you became her burden bearer from the market to the house?"

"No, Mamma. She paid a handcart boy to carry the stuff from the market to the stall at the house. I helped her collect the things she purchased in the market and carried them in crocus bags until she hired the handcart boy. I don't know how she used to manage buying stuff and get them to the cart, before I lived with her and after I left."

Before he could continue with the story, his father chimed in with his comments. "I thought when you left here you were going to learn a trade to better yourself. You said you were tired of chopping wood to burn coal, you didn't like working in the fields, you didn't have the patience to be a fisherman, so you wanted to learn a trade; something like carpentry or masonry so you could make a good living building houses. What happened to those dreams?"

David responded mockingly to his dad. "Ha! Ha! I shed those dreams and woke up to reality. The reality of being exploited and not finding anyone to guide me into the trades or other desirable line of work. That was the well-known reality of Black people's plight that I heard discussed openly by Marcus Garvey supporters. I heard those discussions daily while walking through Parade on the way home from the market. Eventually I woke up to the reality that I was no longer living in Portland, where people looked out for one another. I was living in a place where 'thyman looked after thyself' or be exploited. Contrary to popular beliefs, rich white people were not the only ones exploiting other people. Even Black relatives like aunt Ruby practiced exploitation. She took advantage of me. She did not pay me for my labor. Instead of paying me for the work I did in the market and at home and charge me a reasonable boarding fee, she chose not to pay me at all. Without money, I was tied to her with an invisible rope that prevented me from seeking paid opportunities. I might not have looked like a burden-bearing donkey, but I felt like one, tied to a tree in the pasture. I was not free. The few times I spoke to Victor about his situation, he was not doing well either. We concluded that we were not lazy. If we were given an opportunity, we were willing to work and be paid. But the system of exploitation was stacked against us. So, we decided to join the resistance struggle against exploitation.

Both David's mother and father were shocked to hear his story. Mr. Jones asked, "How does that struggle feed you, put a roof over your head, and raise a family? The few Rasta men we see in Portland do struggle to walk upright and to make sense when they talk after smoking ganga. They struggle to feed themselves with the little money they beg and receive from hardworking people. They like to reap where they have not sown, and the only seeds they planted were not in the ground, but in the young girls they breed. Isn't that what Victor did? How many young girls did you abandon while they were pregnant or as old people use to say, while they were in the family's way?"

Mr. Amos's eyes were blazing with anger as he spoke. Mamma reached out and took his right hand in hers. It was her attempt to keep the conversation going without Papa giving vent to his disappointment with David's apparent failure.

Then she said, "Let's calm down and not allow Satan to get in the midst of this family discussion."

Mr. Jones responded, "You're right, Mama. It's just that I expected David to pick up something other than trash when he went to Kingston."

Harry was not surprised that Mr. Jones was angry with David, but he was not pleased to hear such negative comments about Victor, the father who neglected his mother and her infant son, but whom he was beginning to think of more favorably. He thought if Mr. Jones had the opportunity to relate to kind-hearted Rasta men like Joshua and his son David, he would not be so critical of Rastafarians and may even be more accepting of his son. He was tempted to reveal his Coronation Market experience, David's positive role in rescuing him from that indifferent world, then investing valuable time reconnecting him with family in St. Thomas and introducing him to family he did not know in Portland, without any financial reward. But he was unsure of its possible impact. He quietly consoled himself that his experience with Rasta men were different from David's parents. He hoped that someday, they will learn the truth about their son's kindness.

David picked up the conversation again. He apologized for falling short of his parent's expectation and confessed that the only reason why he did not contact his loving family for many years, was his concern that they would not share his opinions or worse, they may reject him.

He summarized his beliefs by stating, "Black people were stolen from Africa and enslaved by white people. Black people have been fighting for freedom ever since. Unlike Nanny who chopped up white people with her machete right there in Portland, Rasta people are fighting a war of resistance with a different kind of weapon. They are resisting the idea that Black people are inferior to white people. They are resisting the idea that they must continue working like slaves in fields they don't own, in white people's factories and white people's homes. They reject the white man's lie that God is white and partial to the needs of white people. Finally, Rasta believes the ultimate salvation of Black people in Jamaica depends on Black people coming to their senses like the prodigal son and returning to their fatherland in Africa."

After David opened himself to his parents and emptied his ideas in their laps, it was like all nature was listening for him to continue speaking. There was no wind blowing leaves on the trees. Birds that were already perched on the trees were motionless. The bees stopped buzzing, butterflies clung to the pistils of flowers with motionless wings. Even ants stopped crawling. It was the kind of stillness and attentiveness a scout master demanded in a drill exercise when he shouted, "Attention!"

No one listening to David could deny the sincerity of his opinion. But what difference would his sincerity make to his parents? Harry waited to hear Mr. Jones' response. After a long pause, he said, "If you got nothing else from this Rasta doctrine, you learned how to reason and make your point. But there is at least one big problem and related consequences with your idea about Black people coming to their senses. Here is the problem. Who will determine when someone comes to his or her senses? What are possible consequences? When people come to their senses, will they share the same outlook? If their outlook lead people like your brother and sister to England

and Canada instead of the fatherland, who will determine if they came to their senses?"

After those questions, a firefly spark of light pierced the darkness in Harry's head. He glimpsed the following questions shimmering in an enlightened area of his brain. What if everyone lost his way in the darkness of believing that people's actions are usually preceded by careful thought, commonly understood as coming to their senses? But, what if the alternative is true? Real-life circumstances condition people to act impulsively, not thoughtfully? What are the long-term consequences of peoples' thoughts chasing the actions they have already taken?

Despite Mr. Jones' complementary remark about David's reasoning, it's possible that he misunderstood how the experience in Kingston conditioned his son to act. Reasoning may not have been the prelude to David's action, but more likely the justification for actions he took already or to which he was fully committed.

Harry recalling discussions he heard from university students at Parade, thought the following example could help David's parents understand how real-life experiences condition a person to act first and reason after. He said to them, "Imagine David or any young man walking with a girlfriend along the beach on a beautiful moonlit night. Suddenly, the young man comes face-to-face with a dog, growling in a threatening manner with its teeth exposed. The young man's eyes see the danger and automatically call on his body, rather than on his thought to respond. His body's emergency system demands action. In response, his heart beats faster, his muscles become tense, he is sweating, his eyes narrowly focus on the dog, he either feels stronger or weaker. He begins to sweat. If his muscles feel stronger, he will be able to fight. If they don't, flight will be the choice. The decision is not governed by thought because thoughtful examination of alternative actions would be too slow for emergency response. He feels the unstable sand under his feet and his body signaled that it would be impossible for him to sprint fast enough to outrun the dog. So, in a split second his body's mechanical response system chose fight. Had he been thinking, he would have known that he had no weapons except his hands and his feet. Additionally, he had never fought a dog before that day. But even worse, his girlfriend could be a spectator to a calamity if he were overpowered and bitten by the dog. The only scenario in his impulsive response is how to deal with the immediate threat by that dog and not be hurt seriously. His safety and not his girlfriend's is the priority. If running were advantageous, he would run. It would be up to his girlfriend to run as fast as necessary. If he had to fight, he would be fighting for his life. Saving his girlfriend from danger would be an afterthought, not an impulsive reaction to that threat. Now, it has been said that people lay down their lives for others. But in those scenarios, people were able to think before they acted. Those are rarely impulsive actions."

Harry also helped them to understand what could happen if the girlfriend acted impulsively rather than thoughtfully, during the same set of circumstances. "When she realized that she was at risk, her heartbeat also increased. She began sweating and her body, rather than her mind, assessed whether she should fight or run away. She immediately reacted to the threat before her boyfriend did. She grabbed him and used him as a shield to protect her from being bitten by the dog. Her need to survive ranked higher than the safety of her boyfriend whom she made more vulnerable to the dog's attack."

Finally, Harry asked then to imagine David's reactions to his girlfriend after the dog's owner intervened to prevent the dog from attacking them. Then he suggested that both would have experienced the reality of acting impulsively in their individual self-interest. "David would be surprised that his girlfriend's instinct was to use him as a shield during a possible attack by the dog. But David would also have to acknowledge that the actions he contemplated were only in his self-interest."

As interest in the discussion increased, they imagined various every day unplanned actions that narrowly focus on a person's survival, like the scenario of David and his girlfriend did. One scenario imagined that many wealthy people in Kingston and plantation owners in the country, were using instincts rather than thought to justify the process of becoming rich at the expense of others, especially the poor. That's why they are indifferent to poor people, whom they use as shields against various imagined calamities. What is surprising, is the fact that poor people who are left behind on the lower rungs of society's ladder, seem to lose the instinct to act quickly in their own interest. Not only are their thoughtful responses to perceived real threats very slow, but by stifling their God-given ability to counteract repeated threats quickly, their survival is threatened.

Harry concluded his comments by noting, "David and his Rasta brethren realized that engaging the fight in Jamaica against the dominant powers require better weapons. Their current weapons are mere grains of sands against deadly bullets. Their alternative survival strategy is flight, preferably to Africa, where they hope to have a cooperative rather than a blood-sucking relationship with native Black people."

After Harry's comments, David continued the discussion by explaining to his parents, necessary adjustments undertaken by some Black people in reaction to oppression by the ruling class of white people.

"For a long time, Rasta man decided on a strategy of fleeing from Jamaica back to Africa. He even decided which country in Africa is the best place to go. That place is called Ethiopia. It's the home of the King of Kings, Jah Ras Tafari, Haile Selassie, the living God. But talking about going home has not led to definite travel plans. And if there is no travel plan, I-man remains a sufferer in this foreign land. That's why some brethren have started to make adjustment to the ways in which they occupy this country during our sojourn. Many of them started their own business, in resistance to working for the white man. Their business includes the sale of music, carved wood sculptures, rubber sandals from discarded motor vehicle tires, artistic paintings of landscapes and laborers serving time on sugarcane plantations during the hottest season of the year. Instead of them going to people looking for work, people come to them for the products they create. In fact, I am not far from starting on a venture with my brethren Joshua. Thanks in part to little Harry who is present with us today. He reminds us that in the Good Book, my namesake David was the father of Solomon, the wisest man who ever lived. He also reminded us that God demonstrated in his dealings with Solomon, that there is a two-stage process for taking on the challenges of this world. First, seek wisdom from God. After one becomes wise, God gives riches to that person as a kind of wise man bonus. Wisdom before wealth is the proper sequence designed by God for success. You don't have to think long or hard to see that this sequence makes sense. If you are a wise person, you have gained special or general knowledge, which is reinforced by experience and good judgement. Wealth associated with such wisdom is not generally acquired overnight, partly because the success is dependent on your relationship with other people, including partners and supporters. Furthermore, experience taught you that wealth is multiplied when shared, rather than when it is hoarded or simply lavished on yourself.

"Fools who acquire wealth before wisdom, may or may not lavish the wealth on themselves, but more tragically, they lack knowledge and experience to build wealth in a way that benefits other people, some who are poor through no fault of their own. Unfortunately, in Kingston, this lack of sensitivity to the needs of others is not limited to fools who may be rich. It is the core element in most people, who must instinctively guard themselves against crooks. Kingston is not just a difficult place to live, it is a kind of modern-day Babylon that leads many to destruction. People need to find Zion as the alternative destination to Babylon. Zion is both a state of mind and locations all over God's earth where everyone is welcomed. Zion could be England or Canada, where my brother and sister are acquiring wisdom."

By the end of David's speech, everyone was ready for a nightcap. David's mom and dad had white rum, diluted with very sweet lemonade. David made a ganga spliff and quietly smoked it under an ackee tree, a little distance from where Harry was sitting beside his parents. David's mom gave Harry a cup of lemonade with a few drops of rum it. Finally, David shared a few drags of his spliff with Harry.

It was difficult to say how high everyone was before they settled into bed that night. Harry slept like a baby. He did not hear a sound during the night, not even the early morning wake-up call by rooters.

After two days, it was time to say goodbye to David's mom and dad and to Portland. David and Harry did not travel the shorter route through St. Thomas. They did not return to say goodbye to Harry's grandparents. By returning via the Junction route, they avoided the temptation to stop for a visit with Tarta in St. Thomas.

On their way back to Kingston, Harry was seated on the far side of the scenic blue waters of the sea. But on the near side of the road, there were acres of coconut palm trees waving goodbye and ceremonially spinning anti-clockwise when the bus drove by them.

David was quiet and may have been reflecting on the reunion with his family, even while he appeared to be admiring the natural beauty of the receding countryside. Harry was quietly reflecting on David's names. One was David, the beloved son and desirable neighbor in Portland. The other was Barracuda, a man who lives in a hut at the rail yard in Kingston. Barracuda was most likely a nickname that David acquired. But Harry suspected that there was an underlying story behind the nickname. So, he started to search his memory for clues that might reveal the reason for the nickname.

He reflected on underlying stories of nicknames like "Suck finger Jack." That would be the name used to mock a boy who should no longer be sucking his finger at his age. Another was "Sunny Mongoose," the name given to a red-skinned man whose frizzy hair color and undesirable behavior reminded people of a mongoose. (Incidentally, mongoose was a small grizzly-looking ten-pound animal with a large appetite for snakes. It was brought to Jamaica to rid the island of poisonous snakes that were a menace to farmers. But it became notorious for preying on domestic animals, including chickens when there were no more snakes.) Sunny Mongoose, like his four-legged namesake, earned the reputation of being a thief. He was so despised that people would constantly mock him, throw stones at him, or have dogs chase him away from their properties.

The stories Harry heard about barracuda the fish did not suggest a reason for David's nickname. In those stories, this fish was a rare catch. More often than being caught, the barracuda would snatch fishes off a fisherman's hook before the catch could be hauled into the boat. Their demonstrated strength, aggression, and noticeably sharp teeth were fierce weapons that they often used successfully against other animals in the sea or humans who invade their territory. Harry remembered hearing stories about an encounter at Cutter Point, during which one-foot Babbo lost his leg.

It's true that David appears to be strong, but Harry did not find him to be threatening. Although the first time he saw Harry naked on Darling Street, he stated that he was going to grab some clothes for Harry to wear. The determination in his voice hinted that he would do it at any or no cost. Additionally, Ras Joshua said something about Barracuda being a righteous man who will take back what the rich stole from poor people.

After Harry's thoughts failed to find an explanation for David's nickname, he decided to ask David how he got the name Barracuda. David smiled before giving the surprising answer about who gave him the nickname.

He said, "Your father, Victor, gave me that nickname and it has stuck to me like glue." His smile then broke into a laughter that kept punctuating everything he said with loud laughs when he reflected on the incident that led to his new name. "Me and Victor were country boys in Kingston, the equivalent of fish out of water. We had difficulty breathing in that socially suffocating environments, such as the homes of previously unknown relatives like aunt Ruby or the homes of uncharitable so-called friends. Our survival was at risk if we were too slow to develop our ability to help ourselves. We united our efforts as we did previously in Portland, but now in the service of justice and against oppression, as suggested by the new Rasta doctrine. We devoted so much time to the movement, that we barely had time to scavenge for food or huddle with other homeless brethren. My self-appointed job was to identify potential candidates for recruitment and direct them to Victor, whose self-appointed role was a scout. He obtained background information from the recruits and determined their potential contribution to the movement.

"One night I surprised Victor with a potential new convert. The candidate was not the usual bewildered country boy in Kingston. She looked sensible, a very attractive half-Chinese woman, born and bred in Kingston. Victor could not believe his eyes when he saw the attractive woman. He was even more delighted when his evaluation strongly confirmed that the woman was genuinely interested in knowing more about the movement. After the woman departed, with a promise to attend future meetings, Victor was anxious to know how I recruited her."

"What did you say to her?" he asked.

David responded, "I said the same thing to her that I usually say to everyone else I recruit. Well, that's not strictly true. I was inspired to sharpen the argument for this recruit, so I included two quotations from the Good Book that I thought fit the situation, Isiah 62:11 which said, 'Say to the daughter of Zion, behold, your salvation comes,' and 2 Kings 19:21-22, 'This is the word that the LORD hath spoken concerning him; The virgin the daughter of Zion hath despised thee, and laughed thee to scorn; the daughter of Jerusalem hath shaken her head at thee. Whom hast thou reproached and blasphemed? and against whom hast thou exalted thy voice and lifted up thine eyes on high? even against the Holy One of Israel.'

"I then interpreted the Scripture for her, by telling her, the Holy One of Israel is Haile Selassie, Jah Rastafari, the living God. The Scripture predicted that he would be reproached by the virgin daughters of Zion. But Jah wants her to know that salvation is not only for the brothers, but for beautiful virgin sisters of any age, even those who laughed Rastafari to scorn."

Victor found David's serpent-like use of the Scripture to tempt the young woman with the Rasta doctrine very funny. After laughing uncontrollably for several minutes, he slapped David's back and exclaimed, "The old-time story in the Good Book said we must be 'fishers of men,' but like a modern fisherman, you *'overstand'* the importance and the necessity to catch beautiful daughters of Zion also. It gives me great pleasure to invest you with the coveted title, Ras Barracuda."

David attributed the turning point in their recruitment strategy and in their lives, to that event. From then on, it was okay to recruit women and not men only. Additionally, that recruitment strategy had advantages. Unlike male recruits, the women often showed their gratitude in desirable ways; providing occasional cooked meals, periodic shelter, and even companionship.

Harry was still smiling when he arrived in Kingston late that afternoon. He and David wasted no time getting to the rail yard. Apparently, nothing had changed since they left. Joshua was not there, but everything was intact. They were hungry and rushed to buy some spicy veggie patty and coco bread to eat as a quick snack. In fact, Harry bought the snack for both of them with money his grandparents gave him. They ate and awaited Joshua's return to start implementing changes from the train yard to the next phase of their lives.

CHAPTER 8

Enlightenment

Harry anticipated further discussions of three basic issues that would likely guide their activities when he, Victor, and Joshua leave the train yard. First issue would be a working knowledge of wisdom, not clouded by ganga smoke. Second, corrective measures in everyday business activities, without which, some people would be literally and figuratively sleeping in Coronation Market. Third, his future relationship with both men.

His gut told him that any future relationship with those brethren would always be against the backdrop of their extraordinary kindness to him. They helped to reunite him with Tarta and his mother, in a way that ended his obsession to live in the Market under subhuman conditions. They initiated his positive feelings for his father, by telling him stories about Victor's life in Portland and in Kingston. Barracuda reinforced those positive feelings, when he introduced Harry to Victor's parents and siblings in Portland. From his perspective, those men had no obligation to keep him around, especially since he increased their responsibilities and added to their expenses, while giving nothing in return. Even though his dreadlocks made him look like a Rasta, he had been skeptical of the doctrine and had doubts about his commitment to its principles. But if he had to leave them, where would he go? He had an obligation to support Tarta who had grown older, but he was no more prepared to live in the country than in Kingston. He was developing an interest in learning how to break the invisible white man's chain that Tarta spoke about. But he had not progressed to pursuing that interest nor to supporting himself and Tarta.

When Joshua arrived about 7:30 PM, he told Harry and Barracuda that he spent the last few days in the parish of St. Thomas. While there, Jah led him to the new settlement site which he plans to call New Canaan, because it reminded him of the time when God called Abraham from where he was living to settle in Canaan. This New Canaan is on underutilized Crown Lands, neglected by the government. He speculated that Jah may have chosen St. Thomas Crown Lands for three reasons. First, it is next door to Kingston, the commercial center of the island where I-man can sell products from the land. Second, this Crown Land has many acres to spare, because it has the third largest acreage of crown lands in the island, after the parishes of Clarendon and St. Elizabeth. Third, to honor the memory of Paul Bogle who was hanged publicly in the parish capital of Morant Bay, because he demanded better working conditions for poor Black people in that parish.

After reflecting on the fact that Harry knew nothing about Crown Lands, Joshua explained their significance. "Crown Lands include thousands of acres of land that slave masters stole from native people and gave to representatives of the British Crown. But the Crown no longer knows what to do with these lands, so nobody is using them. Jah's solution to that injustice, is to inspire us to occupy a piece of that land near the foot of the Blue Mountain and use it productively. From what I have seen, it is ideal for growing the weed and coffee as cash crops. While we are waiting four years for the coffee to be ready for market, we will make quicker profit from many crops of the weed, which will be ready for harvest every three months. This project will require the kind of hard work that me and Barracuda were accustomed to as younger men, but this time we will be working for ourselves and not for any slave master. I have already enlisted the help of a small group of brethren to help us clear a spot to build our dwellings. That project will take six weeks. Next, we will clear the field to plant ganga in the vicinity of the dwellings and coffee further away. I am willing to invest the seed money to start this project but want to know how you feel about the plan. Are you willing to act on our current belief that with wisdom guiding us, we don't have to leave Jamaica, because Jah will give I-man the riches of the earth wherever we dwell? I have another idea to add to the plan before you answer my question. I believe we must organize ourselves like the pyramids of old in Africa. Start by building a strong foundation on which the next project and even the next generation will succeed. This means that everyone in our organization must have a function like every stone in the pyramid. Some may require chiseling to chip away problems that prevent them from fitting in."

Both David/Barracuda and Harry were surprised at how quickly Joshua decided to implement changes that would ensure his survival in Jamaica, rather than Africa. Even though he asked for their opinion, they felt that their opinions would be like icing on a cake that had been served. While Harry was thinking what to say, Barracuda spoke in support of the project, with recommendations to ensure its success. "Thank you, Joshua, for your quick work in identifying a location for the project and for your financial commitment to its success. The project will be both challenging and worthwhile, so please count on me to support it with every bone in my body. I also support the idea that Black people don't have to move back to Africa to survive, because Jah's blessings are everywhere. I hope the people recruited to participate in the project will be similarly committed to living in Jamaica, rather than in Africa. But I worry that some Rasta recruits may fail to support the project wholeheartedly, because of their commitment to resettling in Africa. I believe the project needs righteous Black people, like the Maroons, who were willing to fight here and now for survival. Let me add, that I will also contribute some money to the project, but I need assurance that there will be enough money to keep the project going until it starts paying for itself. Tell us the background of the people you recruited. How similar are their ideas to our plans? Are their differences small enough to risk working with them? How good are they as team players? Do they share our social concerns for the needs of others? Finally, what is their attitude toward money? Remember, even the white man's Bible states, 'For the love of money is the root of all evil.'"

In his response to Barracuda, Joshua said, "I recruited nine men to join the three of us. I told them that we would not be working for wages each week, but we will share the profits remaining from our expenses after we harvested the crops. The men I recruited are equally persuaded by Garvey's ideas of Black economic empowerment in every part of the world and that God has a special relationship with all Black people. I believed that they have enough in common with you, little Harry, and me that we can work together on the project. The barrack style buildings to be constructed, will provide rough lodgings for twelve of us bachelors, until expanded to accommodate sisters of Zion. One of the recruits is a man that people call Jump-Start. He has a truck in reasonable running condition once it's started. That will be his investment in the project. With his help, we will be able to bring supplies to the compound and move goods to the market. In fact, the number of coconut and breadfruit trees on the property gives us the opportunity to sell two truckloads of these products in Kingston each week."

David/Barracuda again pressed for more clarity with the following suggestions. "There are two types of pyramids. One is the African type you described with a strong foundation to support the rising structures above the base. There is another type that the Bible called the Tower of Babel. In the African tower you spoke about, the stones at the bottom not only withstood the pressures of weight above but pressures from many directions. They also withstood unpredictable destructive natural events like winds and rain. It's important to note that the other tower called Babel, was started, but never completed. I'll tell you why. It is because the people did not speak the same language and could not understand what each other was saying or doing. So, if we don't want to risk building another Babel instead of a tower, we must avoid the risk of speaking multiple languages, but not understanding one another. When it is time to push, we can't afford to have others pulling in the opposite direction because of misunderstanding. The language of success is a magnet that unites us against negative forces that will scatter our efforts. As a practical example, when we decide to plant ganga, we need guidance from brethren who know how to grow that plant, so that we are speaking the same language of success. There are many who smoke the weed but know nothing about the plant. The same approach will be necessary for the coffee project. Additionally, the coffee workers will need renewed inspiration during the four to six years before the coffee is ready for market. I believe we will strengthen the foundation for success by having a group meeting to outline our plans. That meeting will help our recruits understand our plans. It will give us all insight into one another's ability to speak the same language and help our projects withstand various pressures. Maybe it's best to have that meeting before we move to New Canaan. How do you feel about my idea?"

Not surprisingly, Joshua agreed to the meeting. He limited the number of people invited to participate in the project, by holding the meeting in a place that would not attract a lot of attention. He ruled out Parade, because of the many distractions in that park and to minimize the risk of uninvited guests. He also ruled out the rail yard where he slept, because the background noises would be distracting. He decided that the waterfront at Kingston harbor would be a good meeting place. The location was convenient and familiar to those invited and might have a calming effect on people during a contentious reasoning session.

Joshua called the meeting on a Wednesday night. There was no question that Jah Rastafari also accepted the invitation and showed up with the reflection of his illuminating presence on the men's faces. The men saw his presence in the brightness of the full moon, which appeared to be more than a direct reflection of the sun. They saw his presence in the playful twinkle of stars signaling their distant approval and in sounds of gentle waves blending in perfect harmony with the muffled sounds of lovers in the background. Joshua introduced the men individually by their street names before they embraced one another with the ceremonial greeting, "One love." It turned out that the introductions were mainly for Harry's benefit, because the brethren were acquainted with one another, although not to the extent necessary for the project.

Joshua reminded the men of the project's objective. "The goal of the project is to make each of us self-sufficient in Jamaica, not in Africa. Does anyone have a problem with that goal? Going once! Going twice! Sold!"

His next concern was how to achieve the goal of self-sufficiency. "My answer to the challenge of achieving self-sufficiency, is working cooperatively to unshackle ourselves from the tangled webs of white man's financial and demoralizing bondage. In a nutshell, the purpose of this gathering is to discuss what each man will contribute to the project's success.

"Brethren, the time has come for us to rise and shine. I have spoken to you individually about this project before tonight and you gave me your words of support. But as we all know success requires more than words. That's why old people use to say, 'Talk is cheap.' Our discussions up to this moment, focused on the seed time and harvest of two plants, coffee, and the ganga weed. But during a discussion last night, Barracuda wisely suggested that we should have this meeting to discuss the overall needs of this project and what each of us will contribute to its success. This is about working together like the ants. It is about uniting our efforts to do something that no one of us can do alone.

"Let me start with the positives. Jah has given us fertile land, bearing breadfruit and coconuts. It is flowing with water, not milk and honey as in the olden times. Brother Jump-Start is donating his truck to the project and we estimate that he will help to generate income for the project by transporting two truckloads of breadfruits and coconuts for sale in Kingston each week. He will need people to help him reap those crops and transport them to market. I will provide some money to buy material for shelter to protect us from the elements. The project will need carpenters or people with some knowledge of how to put up a house that can withstand the next hurricane. We will jointly improve the living arrangements over time. Barracuda will provide money to buy ganga plants and coffee seeds for the project. He will need people who know how to work the ground, planting seeds and weeding grass. But in addition to those specific tasks, we need a cooperative relationship of pitching in wherever help is needed. So, I would like everyone to share what he intends to contribute to this project and any other idea that he thinks will be helpful."

Ras Israelite took the opportunity to share his opinion. "Joshua, I can't say I know the exact location of this property. But from your description it is probably in the region of Four Miles Wood. This area is not a grassland. As the name suggests, this is a fertile area with very large trees. We will need to do a lot of work cutting down trees before we make a clearing to plant ganga and coffee. So, the way I see this project, you will need much more labor than eleven men and a boy can provide. Now don't get me wrong. If I am correct, this could be additional good news. We have two possible strategies for clearing the forest. One way is to burn it down. But I don't think that is a good idea, because it will attract unwanted attention, and we don't have enough men to control the fire. A better alternative is to burn coal. This will generate income to add to what we make from the sale of breadfruit and coconuts. Additionally, coal could provide steady work for people for a long time and be a reliable source of income for our community. So, here is my question for the group, does anyone know how to burn coal?"

Both Joshua and Barracuda had big smiles on their faces as the group shouted, "Here! Here!"

Barracuda reinforced the groups positive feelings about the project, when he said, "I burned coal for a living as a young man in Portland and would be willing to guide and support others with that project. It will be a reliable source of income so long as people in Kingston need coal to cook their food and country people continue to substitute coal for their wood burning stoves and fire places." After his remarks, Joshua asked Israel what his commitment to the project was.

Ras Israelite said, "Me no have no money fi invest in the project, but I will invest my strength in cutting down trees, making lumber, burning coal, all in gratitude to Jah for giving the group the opportunity to earn a good living. I will also try to raise money to purchase at least one saw big enough for use by a two-man team to cut down big trees."

Stick-Man, who had a reputation for his victorious stick fights, often against more than one opponent at a time, spoke next, "When I heard about the project, I was excited about growing the weed on a big weed farm in the country, far, far, away from Babylon police. Now, according to your plans the weed farm will be delayed indefinitely, until the land is cleared of overhanging trees. I wonder if my wise brethren overlooked the possibility that the overhanging tree branches may be good cover for the delicate weeds. Rather than cutting down the trees before planting the weed, it's possible that we only need to clear the bush from under the tress before planting the weed. So, in addition to helping with jobs specified by the group, I volunteer to clear a patch under the trees, plant a few ganga plants as an experiment, to see if they grow under those conditions." The group welcomed his suggestion and looked forward to the result of his experiment.

Other men in the group spoke quickly and basically echoed previous speakers' thoughts about offering their full physical and moral support, but no financial resources. Only one person among the final group of men, said something different. Not surprisingly, he was Dunce-Man, whose wisdom defied his nickname. He remarked, "The brethren who had their say before me, said nothing about day-to-day living arrangements during the six weeks when we will be building the shelter. Them never talk about where we will sleep during those six weeks, cook food, or empty their bowels. How often will we accidentally step into one another's shit, left randomly in the bushes we are supposed to be weeding? How much time will be lost cleaning shit off our machetes, our shoes, and even our bodies, instead of working on the project?"

After his questions, he suggested two preliminary solutions to the problems he identified. "I believe our first job is to pitch a bamboo tent and cover it with coconut leaves or tarpaulin. If we can't get tarpaulin large enough to cover one big tent for everyone, then let the size of the tarpaulin determine how many tents to pitch. Bamboo can also be used to make sleeping cots, rather than us sleeping on the ground. Second, use voluntary help of a few men to dig a pit for a latrine, followed by others who enclose it with bamboo siding.

I believe those two tasks can be completed on the first day of our arrival. Additionally, those practical accomplishments will confirm our ability to get things done and energize the group for future tasks."

Barracuda complemented Dunce-Man and Stick-Man for their practical suggestions, before offering his contributions. "I'm committed to taking back from greedy rich people our birthrights that they have stolen from us. The reclaim arrangements have been made with brethren on the inside of various wholesale stores in anticipation of this opportunity and the time has come for me to place orders which will include machetes, tree saws, ground forks, shovels, hoes, ropes, nails, hammers, tarpaulin, lanterns, crocus bags to ship breadfruit, bananas, and coal to Kingston. Given the condition of Jump-Start's vehicle and the conditions of the road leading to this compound, I will arrange to have another vehicle make the deliveries as close as possible to the compound. I will rely on Joshua to determine where the drop off should be made and to organize a crew to move items from the drop off location to the compound." His remarks were the final positive contribution to the meeting which left everyone feeling high.

The parting words from Joshua were, "Be ready to journey to New Canaan in two days. We will gather on the eastern side of Parade, facing East Queen Street at dawn."

On the way back to the train yard, Harry asked Joshua if there was a post office near New Canaan, where he could send mail to his mother and Tarta and receive their responses. Joshua understood Harry's seemingly urgent need to re-establish and maintain contact with his mother and promised to find the nearest post office when they moved to the country. He also shared with Harry his opinion that some of the men may not have much interest in a post office for a variety of reasons, including the desire to remain anonymous.

That night, Harry went to bed, but during the brief period of sleep, he had a vision of the invisible chain of slavery that Tarta spoke about. The chain was long but coiled tightly around a Black man's brain to fit uncomfortably into his skull. Its links, both large and small, seemed to have been made of iron and in place long enough to rust. The larger links were wrapped around the outer portion of the brain and wedged in the skull. The smaller links were wedged so tightly into the grooves of the brain that they killed many brain cells and limited the growth of new ones. He was surprised to learn that the chains were no significant impediment to most manual labor, but to higher function learning activities. Additionally, the iron in many Black men's brains was responsive to the white man's magnetic field. But even worse, some Black men were so strongly magnetized that they also became magnetic fields that neutralized independent actions of other Black people.

Harry could hardly breathe when he awoke to thoughts about the challenges of breaking those chains and demagnetizing Black people. He wondered if the move to New Canaan would inspire the men settling in that community to break those invisible chains of slavery. While the relocation puts them out of the range of white people, was distance enough to demagnetize them and break the chains? Would Tarta be satisfied that Harry was learning to break the mental chains, by joining a small group of men committed to make a handful of poor Black people free and prosperous? Will he be disappointed that their plans were not as extensive as those of Paul Bogle, who sought to break the chains for as many people as possible?

Harry reflected on Joshua's preaching at Parade, that people must be their brother's keeper. His model of human success was symbolized by the African pyramid, where every stone in that structure had an interdependent relationship with the other stones. He also reflected on Barracuda's statements about wisdom, that knowing right from wrong is very important and should precede the pursuit of wealth. Finally, before daybreak, he wanted to learn how to make heavy ships float on water, planes fly in the sky without visible support, and how to send messages all over the world with instruments better than the abeng used by the Maroons.

At daybreak Harry opened his eyes and his heart to new possibilities amidst many unanswered questions. In the back of his mind was a lingering desire to fulfill Tarta's wish that he become a person to break the invisible chains of slavery. But his immediate concern was how to get answers from the brethren about their plans, in ways that did not indicate mistrust of their judgement. He started by asking how the new settlement would be different from the communities that Nanny and Paul Bogle lived in.

Barracuda responded immediately, "We are not slaves. We are not in physical bondage. We are free to leave Kingston and move to New Canaan. That difference should not be underestimated. In the old days, slaves did not have the freedom to choose where they would like to live, nor to move from one place to another. In those days they worked for the backra man in exchange for poor food and crude shelter. Today, the playing field is still not level, but is certainly not as steep as it used to be."

Joshua chimed in also, "The twelve of us in New Canaan will be the human seeds in that settlement. We must take root, sprout, and bear fruits. This is not a project that matures overnight. It will require work within our community. But to grow, we will need to keep pace with the needs of others around us, otherwise we become a stagnant pond, a mere breeding ground for mosquitoes and other parasites. You should also know that an important element in building strong bonds in a group like ours, is the respect we show for each other's ideas. That's why I called the meeting at Kingston Harbor and invited everyone to share their opinions about the project and what they intend to contribute. I strongly believe that rubbing one idea against another, is like iron sharpening iron. To remain sharp, we will have to adjust to important changes around us. If we continue to grow chocolate tress after people around us switch to drinking coffee, we will lose business and can blame only ourselves. Right now, people in Kingston have electric lights to dispel darkness and telephone for long distance conversation with one another. By contrast, we will have oil lamps that shine dimly in the dark and we will be limited to speaking with people within the range of our shouting voices. Even if we could use the sounds of the Maroon abeng to send messages, we would be limited to communicating with a few Maroon people who understand those sounds. We grow up hearing that news travel fast, but people in Kingston can prove it. They get their news and current events electronically through a box called rediffusion. We don't have any of that. We don't even have *The Gleaner* nor *The Star* newspapers. Despite these drawbacks, we will need to know what's happening around us and how to react to various changes. Incidentally, the group meeting with the brethren at the pier was a good start in organizing our relationship with one another, but remember that we focused narrowly on work-related activities. That was not an accidental item on the agenda. It was my deliberate effort to start with the least complex problem we will have to solve in building this new community. There are many more activities to be included in future discussions. Harry, I believe Tarta will be proud that you unite your efforts with ours to break the invisible chain of slavery and welcome the spirit of freedom. You have proven to be a keen listener and a thinking young man, so we are relying on you to help us figure out next steps on this journey to freedom."

Harry silently accepted Joshua's compliment and prepared himself mentally for the journey to the country. It was about 4:30 AM when Joshua, David/ Barracuda, and Harry left the train yard with their belongings to meet the brethren at Parade. The clock at Parish Church was striking five o'clock when they arrived. Everyone was on time, except the driver, Jump-Start. Each person was standing beside his belongings in crocus bags on the side walk. From the look on their faces, they were ready for the adventure. They greeted one another verbally, then took turn slapping a nearby gas light post with the palm of their left hands as a way of saying goodbye to Kingston. Soon after, the person responsible for turning off the gas lights around the park began his work. He used a long pole to turn off the lights one by one. The artificial lights were followed by the gentle morning light of dawn. The whistling sound of a peanut vendor's cart pierced the silence on the southern side of the park. They watched as a shadowy figure at the cart, began his day's business of roasting and bagging peanuts for sale later in the day. Finally, a truck with two bright headlights appeared to be slowing to a halt on the east side of the park. The driver was Jump-Start.

The men loaded their belongings in the open back of the truck, after greeting Jump-Start. Joshua joined him in the cab of the truck to guide them to their destination. The men in the back of the truck began swapping stories about their lives in Kingston. They were drawn to Kingston from country parishes by stories of people making money in various ways, other than doing field work. When they arrived, they were fascinated by large numbers of unknown people who knew nothing about them. But they soon found out that anonymity has its drawbacks. First among the drawbacks was the awareness that they had no friends. No go-to person for advice or support. Occasionally, they survived by being cleverer than their competition. But more often, they were the victims of various schemes that robbed them of their money and few possessions. In the spiritual light of the Holy One of Zion, they came to view the economic, political, and spiritual systems as corrupt and took delight in exploiting every opportunity to bring down Babylon. They were not building anything. They were not building families, they were not building villages where people are friendly with one another. They were tearing things down. Their progressive lives were on hold until they unite with their original families in Africa. Even at that time when they were moving away from those experiences, they still felt a rush, thinking about clever ways to destroy Babylon.

Their conversations were interrupted by Dunce-Man who suggested that they don't spend time looking back on the old days, because what happened to Lot's wife could happen to them. They could be stuck in the past, like useless pillars of salt. A new day was dawning, and they needed to wake up to that reality. With that gentle guidance, they shifted focus to their present circumstances. They began to observe the scenery and listen to the cheerful sounds of the countryside. The street lights of Kingston gave way to heavenly lights of the Morning Star and Orion constellation, the group of stars in the Big Dipper. The men admired green trees waving welcome from the hillsides. They enjoyed seeing birds flying overhead and even accompanying them for short distances while doing their morning exercise. They listened as some chirped, whistled, or cooed greetings from their perches on nearby trees. They heard the waves of the sea gently rushing to the shore. They experienced the sights and sounds of nature that were absent, ignored, or buried in their past.

Although traffic on the road was light that time of the morning, Jump-Start resisted the Jamaican tendency to drive the vehicle very fast. He allowed almost every vehicle, except donkey carts, to pass him on the road. He was patient with his truck that sounded like it was groaning from the agony of climbing and descending the hill and gully roads. But he got the men safely to their destination about two hours after they left Kingston.

The men quickly cleared bushes from a site chosen as their meeting place, then formed a circle around the site, while each person gave thanks to the Holy One of Zion for the precious gift of the land and the fellowship of the brethren. That was followed by a hearty meal of sardine, hard dough bread and cream soda, which the brethren acquired the night before leaving Kingston. After the meal the men began cutting bamboo logs from surrounding trees to build structures for tents and a latrine. During their work cutting down the trees, a truck arrived with the supplies that Barracuda ordered. They were particularly happy to receive enough tarpaulin to cover the top of four tents. By the end of their first day, they had accomplished all their planned activities. They built places to sleep and a latrine. During their work together, they increased their bonds of friendship and got to know one another well, even if aliases masked the true identities of some brethren.

Sleep came easily that first night, because everyone was very tired. But Harry was awake to his inner call of finding ways to break the mental chains of slavery. The next evening, he grabbed everyone's attention, when he told them his vision about the invisible chains of slavery in every Black man's head. He also told them that they were all afflicted with the condition and needed to find a cure for themselves and others in their families and villages.

Dunce-Man was the first to acknowledge the importance of Harry's vision, when he said, "The good book said, 'Old men shall dream dreams, your young men shall see visions.' Your vision is truly a fulfillment of Scripture. It demands the little bit of our attention that white people leave us with after many years of abuse. It also demands that we stop being the white man's magnetic fields that extends his ability to neutralize independent actions of other Black people. Brethren, think about this element of the young brother's vision for a moment. The white man has both robbed us of our freedom and used us as his instrument to rob other Black people of their freedom. Let's put the brakes on all plans of going to the white man's heaven or to Africa right now. Let's speed up our efforts to break the chains that bind us to the white man in Jamaica."

Joshua fully supported Dunce-Man's comments by suggesting, "We are the right people, in the right place, at the right time to do what is necessary. I am confident that the white man unintentionally left us with enough common sense to reverse his curse. Let's spend a day thinking about this challenge and meet two nights from today to share our thoughts. But, in the meantime, we should lift our spirits with some weed and seek *overstanding* from the Most High." They agreed with his recommendation and withdrew from one another to commune with the Holy One of Zion.

A heavy shower of rain in the afternoon of the next day, short-ened that day's work activity. But not before the men cut down some trees and selected a place to burn charcoal. That unexpected recess allowed them more time to discuss solutions to the puzzles of men-tal slavery. Stick-Man started the discussion by recalling Joshua's ser-mons at Parade about the white man Cain who was able to kill his brother and had the gall to tell Jah say him was not his brother's keeper. He concluded his remarks with the words, "We will begin to break the chains of slavery when we become our brother's keeper."

Jump-Start was the next to speak. But before he uttered a word, the brethren began to giggle, because of the relationship between the man and his truck. The nickname Jump-Start was meant to mock the way Henry started his truck. He routinely got in the cab of the truck, turn the unresponsive ignition switch several times before getting out to fetch a spare battery from the back of the truck to boost the installed battery. To onlookers, if the installed battery in the truck could not provide power to start the motor, the ignition system, and the lights, it needed to be replaced. But to Henry, if that battery had a residue of juice, he was determined to boost the battery until he drained the last drop of energy from it. Only then would he discard the old battery. He was as patient with the gigglers as he was with his truck. When the men settled down, he said, "My truck has three speeds and I negotiate each speed with either a first, second, or third a gear. I shift into first gear, the slowest and strongest gear, to move the truck initially. After it gathers speed, I shift into other gears, using different combination of power and speed necessary for the road condition. That's why a good driver not only keeps his eyes on the road, he also listens to the sound of the engine telling him when to increase the power of the lower gears or the speed of the higher gears. If this group were a truck, I would say the battery has enough juice to start the motor. But much more is needed to move the truck forward.

"Energy must flow from our charged battery through ignition switch, distributor, spark plugs, and pistons to move the truck. Additionally, all parts must function as a unified system. Any dysfunctional part; the battery, the ignition switch, the distributor, or the spark plugs will prevent this truck from starting and from moving. Brethren, if this group were a truck, what will we do to ensure that it is firing on all cylinders? Who is the battery? Who is the ignition switch, the distributor, the spark plugs, and the pistons? Finally, if this group were your truck, what is your backup plan to jumpstart it when the battery fails?"

The men stood up and applauded Jump-Start's remarks and from that day forward, when the brethren said Jump-Start, they said the name respectfully rather than derisively.

Barracuda was the first person to respond to Jump-Start. "You got that right, brother, when you said our battery has enough juice to start the motor. I can also answer your question about our backup plan. Hear me now! We will never need to jumpstart our engine. It will never fail, because Jah is the everlasting source of our energy when we are connected to him. Secondly, to ensure that we are firing on all cylinders, we need to have the right connection with one another. Jah already said in the Good Book, 'I am the vine, you are the branches. He that abideth in me and I in him, the same bringeth forth much fruit: for without me ye can do nothing. John 15:5.'"

Dunce-Man chimed in, "I am a practical man who deals with specifics rather than generalities. What is our goal other than escaping from Babylon and occupying this promised land? What are our defined responsibilities that Barracuda spoke about? Do we limit those responsibilities to ourselves? Do we take on the larger responsibility of breaking the mental chains of slavery within us, within our brothers and sisters? Let's get down to some specifics."

It was now Joshua's turn to reach for the specifics that Dunce-Man requested. "A wiser man than me said we all go through progressive stages of development ranging from dependence to interdependence. Many, if not all of us, will acknowledge that human phase of dependence on parents and others lasted too long. Among so-called lower animals, dependence on parents ends at birth or after a few months. But Black people's development has been delayed and deformed by prolonged dependence on slave masters. Now that we have broken our outward chains of dependence on slave masters by moving to New Canaan, we have relaunched our independence. Our next step is to choose the objectives we will pursue. I'm happy that we have already organized ourselves into groups to work a portion of the land and generate income to support ourselves. In the coming months we will work together to fully occupy this land and increase its productivity and our income. With your approval, I appoint Barracuda to manage the business of utilizing the land, selling the crops, paying the expenses, and distributing the profit to us. This is a very big job and he may need to call on various people for help.

"I would also like to deal with another set of issues that both Jump-Start and Barracuda compare to parts of a truck engine working together to move the truck. The spark plug has its own integrity, but it must also be able to receive energy from the distributor and pass it on to the pistons. That external relationship between the spark plug interacting with the distributor and the piston is called interdependent relationship. It is a more advanced relationship than independence, because it does more than simply focus on itself. But if we were a truck, I see two phases to our interdependent relationships. One phase is the more obvious interdependence among group members, that old people described as one hand washing the other. The other phase is less obvious, but it is very essential to the integrity of each individual member. It is interdependence of all elements within everyone, that enables that person to be authentic. To be truly himself and herself, rather than a foolish poppy show.

"I can see Dunce-Man applying his practicality to this assignment of interdependence among group members, to ensure that we work together and achieve the objectives we agree on. With your approval, I appoint Dunce-Man to help us achieve those objectives. The second part of this interdependence idea takes us on an inward journey to break the chains of mental slavery. We can never be truly interdependent, if we are restrained by the rusting chains of slavery in our brains that Harry saw in his vision. So, I am calling on the youngest visionary among us, to take us on that inward journey of breaking the invisible chains of slavery."

Then turning to Harry, Joshua said, "This is something your great-grandfather Tarta, still hopes that you will do, and we want to help you do it. I'm even thinking that after we develop the internal and external interdependent relationships in our group, we have an obligation to teach the concepts to our brothers and sisters in the surrounding community. That's one way in which we will be following in the noble footsteps of Paul Bogle, whose untimely death prevented him from breaking the chains of mental slavery. Here is my final thought for the moment. We can learn important lessons from lions, the so-called king of the jungle. With few exceptions, they live in groups called prides. They complement one another's hunting ability and successfully prey on animals much larger than themselves, because of their coordinated group attack. Brethren, we are descendants of the Lion of Judah, Haile Selassie, Rastafari. We are members of a noble pride. Let's not be victims any longer, but noble hunters, coordinating our skills in ways that conquer New Canaan and make it a worthy example, not only in the parish of St. Thomas, but in Jamaica."

Joshua's assignments were approved by the group and the three men willingly accepted their new challenges. Barracuda informed the brethren that he welcomed their ideas on how to make the land more productive and he emphasized the distinction between hard work and productive work, when he said, "There is no shortage of hard work in New Canaan. We will never be laid off from it. But we will need to be smart workers and not slaves. In addition to cutting down a few trees, clearing a small portion of the land, and tilling it with

ground forks to plant ganga and coffee, we need a strategy to cultivate as much of the property as possible. For example, it's possible to
till more of the land with one or two donkeys pulling plows, than all
of us using ground forks. This arrangement would allow most of us
to spend time planting and tending the growing plants. I will be the
first to acknowledge that ploughs are not cheap, but are an investment worth considering as soon as possible. Then after the land is
ploughed, the rest of us can devote our efforts to planting, nurturing
the plants, and reaping the crops. All of us will be tired at the end of
each day, but we will be greatly rewarded for our work."

Dunce-Man also pledged to do all he can to maintain harmony
among the brethren. He then reflected on his experience at Back-A-
wall in West Kingston. "Looking back on those days, I am surprised
by the apparent lack of envy among poor brethren at that place. Some
would say those people had so little that there was nothing worth
envying. Secondly, there was no obvious contempt for one another,
maybe because we were all so low that no one was consciously below
another. We did not even feel competitive with one another, even
though there was a daily struggle for food. But with no storage facility, it made more sense to share food with one another than to hoard
it and let it rot. Now we are in a different place. We are about to start
a voyage in a kind of row boat to an uncharted destination. With Jah
as our pilot, we will get there much faster when we row in unison."

Harry felt some compulsion to say something after the other
men spoke. But it was apparent that he had not quite sorted out his
thoughts. He began haltingly by thanking Joshua for choosing him
to fulfill Tarta's hope of breaking the invisible chains of slavery. He
then acknowledged his indebtedness to both Joshua and Barracuda.
Pointing to them, he said, "Without the friendship of these two men,
I may not be alive today. They not only rescued me from the perils
of Coronation Market, where busy buyers and sellers despised my
nakedness and ignored my hunger, but they united me with my family in St. Thomas, Portland, and England. I am living proof that their
kindness transformed me.

"I share Dunce-Man's opinion that our outward journey is
uncharted, but I believe our inward journey is also uncharted. Each

of us will have to be pioneers searching for our true selves in the rubble of our shattered lives. That search will make inward journey even more difficult, because we will encounter ourselves as both higglers and buyers in various markets, striving to satisfy our greed rather than our needs. We will have to learn how to be acceptable in our own eyes after being brainwashed to be more acceptable in the eyes of others. Hopefully, self-acceptance will be a master key available to each of us with the desire to unlock the rusting chains of slavery tucked away in our brains."

CHAPTER 9

The Promised Land

Two weeks after arriving in New Canaan, Joshua, Jump-Start, and Harry set out to explore the surrounding neighborhood. They were curious about who were their neighbors, where they could buy food that they did not produce or other necessary items before the next trip to Kingston. They also set out to find a post office to mail letters and receive responses from Harry's mother, Tarta, Lucy, and his grandparents in Portland.

Their first stop was at a village called Gap. It's about five miles from New Canaan. Its name may have been coined by someone surprised to find an unusual valley in such a mountainous area near the Blue Mountains. The rugged road leading to the village was not inviting, but the villagers were. They acknowledged our presence with their friendly gestures of both waving to us from their yards and shouting friendly hellos.

A curious older man greeted Joshua, "Wha a gwan Rasta? What bring you to this part of the country? My name is Ralphy, but most people call me Science-Man."

Joshua responded, "One love, Science-Man. These are my brethren, Jump-Start and Harry. We just move into the area and need to find a food shop and post office. Where can we locate these things?"

"Well, Gap is a small community where people don't spend a lot of time writing to anyone. So, it would be a waste of government money even to set up a little postal agency, much less a post office in this community. The nearest post office is in Yallahs, but the grocery store is down the road. You will see it on the right-hand side. It's more a convenience store than a grocery store, because we grow most of our food and raise livestock for fresh meat, we have very little need to buy food there. Although like all Jamaicans, sometimes our taste buds call for mackerel and banana, ackee and salt fish, so when we get that call, we shop for salt-tings in that store. You will find that its business is mostly hardware products and liquor."

"Would you mind telling us why people here call you Science-Man?" Jump-Start asked.

"Well, the simple answer is that people in this village rely on my recommendations of herbs to treat various sickness. It will take a long time to tell you how I got interested in the curative power of herbs. Suffice it to say, I have cultivated an interest in the medicinal power of plants like Guinea Hen Weed, Cerasee, and Feva Grass over many years. If it's God's will, I may even find a herb to curb people's hard-heartedness toward one another. This herbal cure I'm thinking about needs to do more than make people feel high. It must do something good to their hearts."

Joshua and his friends felt good vibrations from Science-Man and thanked him for his hospitality. They proceeded to the convenience store to explore the variety of items that may be useful in an emergency. They confirmed Science Man's assessment of the store, but left there without buying anything, followed the circular road back to where they entered the community, then moved on to find the post office in Yallahs.

Harry felt very happy to reach the post office and mail the letters he wrote. He sent one to his mother with the promised photograph of himself as well as a hopeful story about his adventures with new friends. He also sent letters to Tarta and Lucy, that included directions to New Canaan and plans for developing the property.

They returned from Yallahs with enough grocery to last for a week, then joined the other men at work in the field. They did not

have to report to an overseer as people do when they work on plantations. They worked in their own interests and spontaneously invested
enough time each day to achieve the desired success.

The work day was at least seven hours between seven to twelve
in the morning and two to six in the afternoon. The schedule was
advantageous to working conditions in that location, which was
at a higher elevation and cooler than Kingston. Additionally, they
finished the field work early enough to socialize with one another,
through reasoning sessions.

Before dinner that evening, Dunce-Man suggested a routine to
reinforce Joshua's idea that they were a noble pride from the Lion of
Judah. It required them to make roaring sounds like a lion, in four-
part harmony. The sounds would be joyful, not distress signals. The
entire roar would last two minutes. But between each ten-second
r-o-a-r, there would be a five second-interval. They would determine
the pitch for the roar by tapping the lower portion of an empty drum
pan outside the tents. The harmonious roar would serve two other
meaningful purposes. It would be a symbolic prayer of gratitude for
the bountiful property and a grace for the food they were about to
eat. It became a way of transitioning from physical labor in the field
to enriching their spirits with social activities.

After dinner they sat in a circle, shared a chilung pipe and
mellow reasoning ideas with one another. Harry began the session
of inner exploration, by soliciting ideas from the brethren about
breaking the chains of slavery embedded in their brains. Dunce-
Man was the first to offer his opinion. "One way of breaking the
chains of slavery embedded in our brains is to reject the slave manual that Christians call the Bible, because it teaches obedience
to those calling themselves masters. As a Rasta Man, I currently
believe I am God's special delivery to this world. I was delivered
with Black skin, wooly hair, flat nose, and thick lips. That's only the
outer part of me. Internally, I have much in common with people
of every nation. With that knowledge, I am grateful for the person I
am. I don't harbor emotional attachments to an ethnic ideal person
of any race, because I could be left with inner concerns rather than
inner satisfaction."

Jump-Start chimed in with his support of Dunce-Man's idea. "I totally agree with the point you make about being grateful for who we are. But I hope we don't underestimate envy's historic role of creating personal dissatisfaction with who we are and what we possess. White people in Europe envied the riches of Africa and ruthlessly acquired it, while despising the physical appearance of Black people. By contrast, Black people envied the appearance of white people and accepted the false idea that white appearance was the result of evolutionary superiority. With that misunderstanding, Black people traded their wealth and their people for the unattainable ideal appearance of white people. Even now in Jamaica, Black people are still trading their wealth and their labor for very little more than association with light-skinned people. An important element of envy is that it not only judges something to be valuable, but it creates an urgent need to acquire the envied object. If that envy lock is on those rusting chains in our brains, self-acceptance, yes, gratefulness for who we are could be the master key for that lock."

Ras Israelite spoke next. "Can someone help me understand where to draw the dividing line between envy and desired improvement? This is my concern about the dividing line. Let's say I visited someone's house that had conveniences like running water and electric power, and I desired similar facilities in my house, would my desires be considered envious?"

Stick-Man responded, "In my opinion, envy does more than simply desire the conveniences you admired in another person's house. It also strives to deprive the envied person of his conveniences. Envy does not believe in what old people use to say, 'Live and let live.'"

Hopeton who had not spoken much before, said a mouthful. "The people in this group who know me well, understand that I'm a roots man. My roots are not stringy fibrous roots like grass roots, content to draw nourishment mostly from surface soil. I am a taproot kind a guy. My mind is a big central root delving deep into the soil of knowledge with a compliment of smaller roots, searching for information to nourish the spirit. My digging revealed that all human life started in the motherland of Africa. That's why I agree with Dunce-

Man that differences in humans are largely superficial. For example, we in the Rasta community yearn to return to Africa. But so are people in the rest of the world. Some go back for gold, diamonds, oil, human, and exotic animals. From my viewpoint, Africa continues to give life to the world. But there is an interesting exception in a place called the Dead Sea. This unique body of water is so much lower than the surrounding landscape, that it has no outflow. Evaporation is the only outlet for the water it receives daily. The water remaining after evaporation, turns into dead salt, which does not support life. Nothing but salt grows there. The Dead Sea is an object lesson for me. I see a similarity between white enslavement of Black people and the Dead Sea. Slave masters shoved slaves to the lowest depth of their social arrangements of daily brutalization, that slaves had no outlet for frustration, nor opportunity to grow. Many of their souls dried up under the heat of harsh punishment and isolation from the rest of the world. Their development arrested, their spirit suffocated and died, instead of growing. With the limited freedom we now experience, it is in our interest to break the chains of isolation that restricts us from seeing anything but our surroundings and shadows of the past. Let's use the past as a springboard to the future. Nanny and Paul Bogle left us their examples of seeing futures that would be different from their past. Nanny saw freedom for the Maroons and fought for it in their locality. Paul Bogle's had larger vision that included Black sufferers in St. Thomas and other parts of the island. Whatever we end up striving for, increased knowledge of the world, not only of Africa, must be included. Remember now, knowledge is the white man's most successful weapon against us."

At the end of Hopeton's comments, Stick-Man who was holding the chilung pipe, put out the fire on the weed and rested the pipe on the ground. He said, "Brethren, this speech gives me the biggest high I experienced in a long time. Thanks, Roots Man." Everyone else simultaneously shouted, "Here! Here!"

The next speaker was Zulu. "I heard the Good Book described earlier as a slave manual. But I believe it also contains pearls of wisdom like 'My people perish for lack of knowledge.' To me, Hopeton was saying the same thing as the Good Book, but with a twist.

Knowledge of the past will only get us part way on our journey. To get beyond that break point, we need present-day knowledge of modern development. For instance, imagine a man coming from country parishes to Kingston for the first time and see hundreds of people being transported by rapid means of transportation rather than donkeys. Also, imagine his surprise at the variety of jobs that have nothing to do with working on plantations. This new reality will confirm gaps in his knowledge. But he will not close those knowledge gaps by simply being aware that the gaps exist. He must erase ignorance with new knowledge or perish socially and financially."

Delroy's comments added an element to knowledge that was not previously discussed. "I have heard people say knowledge is power, but we have been discussing knowledge and said nothing about power, other than associating ourselves symbolically, with the mighty Lion of Judah. It's worth noting that the lion is not the largest wild animal. But he is among the most powerful. Secondly, lions use their power when necessary, that is to get food and protect the pride. They do not use their power to kill unnecessarily. If we truly embrace the lion symbol, we will empower ourselves to break any and every chain of slavery that threatens the development and safety of our family."

At the end of Delroy's comments, Joshua inquired if the brethren needed to quench their thirst with coconut water. But the men chose to continue the discussions.

"My nickname is Quiet-Man for a reason. I am a man of few words. I do more listening than talking. But after listening to this discussion, I find myself wondering why we have not discussed money. Where I come from, people say there are two sides to every coin. One side is need, the other side is greed, depending on how it is used. When it's used to satisfy our needs it's a blessing, but when it's used to satisfy our greed, it's a curse. My question to you, brethren, is this, who sets the boundaries between people's need and their greed? Who determines when the boundary is crossed?"

Barracuda responded, "Your question reminded me of the following quotation by Shakespeare in my elementary school reading book, 'There is nothing either good or bad but thinking makes it so.'

But I have moved on from that neutral idea to my current belief that some things are inherently bad. One bad thing is slavery, another relates to the use of money. Given the fact that money is nothing more than a neutral instrument, it can be and is frequently used by people to acquire good things like food and clothing or bad things like poison to kill someone. Unlike money, which can be used for either good or bad purposes, slavery is inherently bad. For example, slave owners used Black people in Jamaica as disposable instruments to extract wealth from sugarcane, banana, and coconut plantations. But before these human instruments were disposed of, they suffered and endured cruel working conditions which slave owners considered insignificant and irrelevant to desired profits. Dehumanizing people is fundamentally evil. Remember now, instruments, human and non-human, are only useful if they satisfy specific objectives. When they no longer satisfy those objectives, they are discarded like worthless trash. Today, discarded human instrument are not restricted to plantations. They are all over the island, including various parts of Kingston. You will see many people languishing on sidewalks. Some are so far along in their deterioration that they have lost the instrumentality to beg. Yes, these are prevailing conditions even today in a so-called free society, where powerful people establish their own boundaries without significant challenge. Now, it is possible to see New Canaan as an instrument, because it is our means to achieving the good things we desire for ourselves and those with whom we are privileged to share. Note that I said privilege to share, not opportunity to show off."

As the evening wore on, long shadows of trees were diminishing with reduced light of the setting sun. The delicate glow of moonlight lit some men's faces more brightly than others. There were fewer bird songs, but louder sounds of crickets. There was the magical light of fireflies challenging us to guess where they would shine next. But the brethren gave no indication that they were weary and tired of the discussions.

Joshua had been listening attentively to the other brethren. He not only digested their opinions but integrated what he heard in his feedback to the group. "During Harry's first trip to Parade with me, we talked about Coronation Market being a place where people buy and sell produce. I told him that people who had nothing to sell nor money to buy, were in the wrong place. That's why when higglers and buyers saw Harry sleepwalking totally naked in broad daylight, it did not occur to them that he was a worthwhile human being. They saw him as instrumentally useless. They felt no desire to feed or clothe him. But here is the newsflash for this evening, many poor people are similarly perceived to be useless and irrelevant as Harry was. They are seen that way by those desiring to be wealthy and by wealthy people who control access to distribution of money in the larger economy. Despite their efforts, the struggling poor are sleepwalking in the universal coronation market place. It's worth noting, that market has expanded beyond buying and selling agricultural products. It now includes increasing varieties of manufactured products to tempt and satisfy people's needs and vanities. Those who have lost the instrumentality to buy or sell in that extended market are overlooked or ignored while sleepwalking in plain sight as Harry did. We, here, as descendants of the Lion of Judah, must break the chains that bind us to various forms of negative instrumentality, while robbing ourselves and others of humanity."

That night when the discussion ended, the men's faces reflected the luminance of moonlight, starlight, and the flickering lights of fireflies. But less obvious were their minds which were now reflecting the luminance of enlightened ideas exchanged during their discussion. As God's special gift to the world, they could be grateful for who they were. They could desire improvement without envy and limit the use of power against defenseless people. They could pursue knowledge, both past and present, to improve their versatility and protect themselves from wanton cruelty, by those who would use them as disposable instruments to satisfy selfish desires.

No one went to sleep on the ideas inspired by that night's reasoning session. All were awake to various possibilities of extruding the chains of slavery from their brains. For Hopeton, it was possible to dig deep into the soil of knowledge with the aid of correspondence courses offered by British colleges. His preferred interest was mathematics, which he called the science of truth. Its language avoids the ambiguity of English double-talk by using unambiguous symbols of circles, triangles, and other geometric figures that reportedly served the ancient scientist, Galileo, well.

Barracuda revised his plans for using a donkey drawn plough to till the soil. He would substitute a tractor with a plough, because it would increase efficiency and versatility to plough the field and haul wood to the kiln to be converted to charcoal. Additionally, it would enable Jump-Start to teach the brethren how to operate the tractor and increase their versatility on the farm. Joshua embraced the possibilities of men with families and bachelors inhabiting the farm, because the land was large enough to have separate houses for each family unit. Additionally, it would have a safe playing field for children, isolated from the dangers of a pasture with ferocious bulls. Families would be united by interdependent needs in many ways that leave greed to die in isolation. Dunce-Man saw the merit of spreading their development strategy to surrounding communities to inspire imitation rather than envy.

Stick-Man announced good news about his experiment with the ganga plants and invited everyone to see the evidence the next day. "Didn't I tell you the weed could grow in the shade? When you finish eating, come look at my truth staring you in your face from the ganga patch. But even though I proved that the weed can grow in that spot, I think it's too easy for the public to see. We need to hide the farm behind the other cultivation. Outsiders, who may include Babylon police, should only see the coffee, banana, and other plants that are legitimately sanctioned. Jump-Start has been teaching me and Quiet-Man to operate the tractor, so I will voluntarily use the tractor to plow the area you brethren choose to cultivate the wisdom weed."

Harry was ambivalent about future possibilities. He contemplated reuniting with Tarta and Lucy, but not on the plantation where they lived. He struggled to find easy answers to several questions in his mind related to their needs. Would they be willing to relocate? Would they adjust easily to the loss of old friends and the newness of strangers? How could he assure Tarta that pride in African heritage and the desire to break the mental chains of slavery, would continue to be at the front and center of his mind for as long he lived? He wanted to unite with his mother living in England, without losing the cherished friendship of Ras Joshua and Barracuda who rescued him. He would like to meet his father and listen to the explanation of why he abandoned Virginia and her infant son. But he would also like to thank his father for the unintended legacy of old friendship with David that indirectly contributed to his rescue from Coronation Market and his new perspective on life.

CHAPTER 10

The Knowledge Key

After that satisfying night of reasoning, Harry felt more comfortable in his assigned role of leading the brethren on their inward search for the chains that bind them and other Black people to slavery. He was drawn to Hopeton's idea that knowledge remains white man's most effective weapon against Black people; but in the right minds, it could be an instrument for good. He was also encouraged by the brethren's spontaneous participation in the discussion and grateful for the rich ideas they contributed. But he was rightly concerned that his quest for knowledge would be thwarted by absence of schools and competent teachers. Rather than trying to solve those problems by himself, he discussed his concerns with Hopeton, who used to take classes from an overseas school. "Hi, Hopeton, the reasoning session earlier this evening left me really thirsty for knowledge. I can hardly wait to go back to school. But since we don't have any schools in the surrounding area, I am thinking of taking correspondence courses. What's the name of the school from which you took your courses? What subjects did you take?"

"My favorite subjects were mathematics and science, but right now I don't remember the name of the school. It will come to me by tomorrow," replied Hopeton.

Harry continued, "In addition to the school in which you registered to take your subjects, I heard that there are many schools in England that offer correspondence courses in various subjects. Are you interested in resuming your studies? If you are, both of us should register for overseas courses and have the material sent to us at the post office in Yallahs. We will have to carve out time from our busy work schedule in the field to study, but we will have opportunities to reinforce our learning by sharing information with each other and teaching interested brethren."

Not surprisingly, Hopeton responded with enthusiasm. "I love it! I love it! After I finished elementary school and ran up against insurmountable barriers blocking my entrance to high school, one of my former teachers blessed me with the knowledge of a British correspondence school, in which I could enroll and take various subjects, just like I was in a traditional school. The nice thing about that idea, was that if the school were reputable, their teaching would be comparable to the best Jamaican high schools, or even our university at Mona. Not long after I registered and started classes. But I had to stop my studies, because I no longer had a permanent address to receive the instructions, nor funds to pay the fees. The arrangement here in New Canaan will provide both money and a stable address."

The next day, Harry told Joshua and Barracuda about the previous day's discussion with Hopeton, that included taking correspondence courses during their spare time. He continued, "Jah must have been listening to my conversation with Hopeton, because His Spirit guided me to a part of the good book that I never read before. It says in Hosea 4:6, 'My people are destroyed for lack of knowledge; because you have rejected knowledge, I will also reject thee.' That passage was followed by words of the wisest man, Solomon, in Proverbs 1:7, 'The fear of the Lord is the beginning of knowledge.'"

Joshua responded, "If Jah is calling you to lead us to the fount of knowledge, heed his call. We will follow and hopefully drink from the fountain also. In addition to the name of a school that Hopeton remembers, we can get a list of overseas schools from the famous bookstore on Harbour Street, in Kingston. We can also get information from your parents, Virginia and Victor, who live in England."

Not long after Harry's discussions with Hopeton, Joshua, and Barracuda, word spread to other brethren, some of whom also indicated interest in joining Hopeton and Harry in the quest for knowledge. Those brethren identified themselves as members of the Knowledge Club. But before a school was selected or anyone registered in it, everyone had to wait for a joint recommendation from Hopeton and Harry, who assumed the task of comparing the teaching reputation, students' success rates, and costs of the courses in various schools. During several weeks of heightened interest in acquiring knowledge, the men continued doing what old people use to say, "Make hay while the sun shine."

More good news came from other brethren. One said, "Last week we met our target of burning over a hundred bags of coal in the kiln. That should be more than enough to put a decent amount of loose change in everyone's pockets."

Barracuda added, "We planted coffee throughout half of the land, with supplemental labor, recruited by Science-Man in the neighboring district of Gap."

During several months, Joshua's prolonged strategy of internal and external development began to take shape. External development focused on achieving financial self-sufficiency by wisely cultivating the land with products that were in demand, but with limited concerns about the law cracking down on the ganga farm. The brethren were careful not to draw attention to the fence that separated the ganga farm from remaining portions of the farm. But as the demand for workers increased, it became necessary to use only the brethren for the sacred tasks of planting the seeds, tending the young plants, reaping the harvests, and selling the weed. They even started to manufacture herbal remedies and other by-products of the weed, rather than selling the entire harvest wholesale. Ironically, the increased availability of authentic high-quality weed did not seem to increase the men's over-reliance on its stimulating properties.

Neighbors recruited to work on other areas of the farm were not only carefully chosen, but indoctrinated with ideas of being chosen by Jah as living example that Black people can work together and succeed in achieving their desired endeavors without being submissive to the will of white people. The indoctrination was intentionally done without coercion during socializing events like lunch breaks, after-work reasoning, and celebrations of Rastafari's gift of spirituality and wisdom to humanity, especially the most recent descendants of mother Africa. Although the reasoning sessions seemed spontaneous, the brethren recognized that Dunce-Man was guiding the discussions, in accordance with his assignment from Joshua, to build the external community.

Under Harry's leadership, strategies for internal development that would unlock those embedded slave chains in the heads of the New Canaan community were also progressing. Information from the Kingston Book Store, confirmed that International Institute of Learning was the name of the correspondence school Hopeton remembered. It also included a list of recommended schools in England, including London University and Cambridge University. Hopeton remained interested in subjects taught by Jamaica technical schools, while Harry's interest was more general. Both of them settled on applying for high school level courses through an external program at Cambridge University, because it offered a variety of subjects related to physical, life, earth, space, and human development. An added benefit of the program was the feedback from personal tutors about what was satisfactory, what was not, and the necessary steps for improvement to pass the exams.

Hopeton enrolled in two courses, algebra and natural sciences. Harry enrolled in Algebra and social sciences. Given their enthusiasm to learn, they invested many hours before dawn and midnight studying the information and answering the questions. They reviewed each other's answers to the algebra questions and benefited from the secondary review, before mailing their answers to the school. As time went on, Hopeton and Harry convinced the other brethren that their studies required more time off from working in the field. The discussion began one evening after work when Hopeton said, "I want to bring something to your attention. The correspondence courses that me and Harry are taking is hard work. It is sometimes harder than fieldwork, even though you can't see the sweat pouring out of our brains like it does on our faces. We would benefit from investing a little more time laboring with the books and less time in the fields."

Harry agreed immediately by saying, "Hopeton took the words out of my mouth. Brethren, this is a very important request. I would even go a little further than Hopeton to say our extra study time will be another form of investment in enriching this community. The time we invested in our studies so far is paying off. Each of us has passed four subjects at the GCE level and almost qualify to begin university studies. Hopeton passed Algebra, Natural Sciences, English, and Calculus. I passed English, Algebra, Economics, and bookkeeping."

The brethren shouted in unison, "Here! Here!"

Joshua complemented them by saying, "You have shared your knowledge generously with all of us and specifically with brethren in the Knowledge Club. You have inspired a few people who have also been bitten by the learning bug. The latest rumor said Stick-Man, Dunce-Man, and Jump-Start passed a few subjects taught by those correspondence courses also. This may even come as a big surprise to everyone, as old as me and Victor are, we believe we could follow your examples. We will be deciding soon what to study. I love reading and I am more inclined to reasoning rather than calculations, but I am willing to try anything that will dislodge the slave chains from my brains and replace them with knowledge-based wisdom. So, I recommend the following compromise to you brethren; excuse both Harry and Hopeton from working in the field on Mondays, in exchange for each of them teaching the subjects they passed. Their classes are to be taught on Saturdays to interested brethren. The duration of the sessions should be approximately one and a half hours." Then turning to Hopeton and Harry, he continued, "Young men, if no one shows up for your classes, we won't hold that against you."

Again, the brethren expressed approval by shouting, "Way to go. Big up, Harry! Big up, Hopeton!" Big up the Knowledge Club!"

The overall transformation of the village was more obvious than the educational accomplishments of men in the Knowledge Club. It was now a settled community, supported by a thriving agricultural foundation and a rich fellowship of brotherhood. The coffee trees were not yet mature to bear fruits, but the compound had fourteen adjoining houses, one for each member of the group and two set aside for guests. It also had a large community center for spiritual reflections and social activities. All the houses were built with the sturdiest lumber from the property.

On a cool Saturday evening in October, following the agreement with Harry and Hopeton, the men assembled for the three-year celebration of their move from the valleys of Kingston experiences to higher levels of personal accomplishments in the remote country village of New Canaan. They cooked three large pots of thick Congo peas soup spiced with scallion, hot country peppers, and thyme. The soup included hard food like sweet potatoes, sweet cassava, coco, and small cylindrical white flower dumplings called spinners. The beverage was coconut water, the desert was ripe naseberries.

After the meal, Joshua said, "Brethren, let's once again give thanks to the Most-High for leading us to this place. Jah continuously blessed us with harmony in our relationships and rewarded us with financial success for our hard work. We had scary moments, one of which was when Jump-Start's vehicle collided with a drunken man's truck. As you know, Jump-Start was driving on the left side of the road at the nine-mile stretch from St. Thomas to Kingston. With the steering wheel on the right side of the vehicle, he had an unobstructed view of the approaching truck attempting to overtake a donkey cart before passing Jump-Start. The oncoming driver barely passed the cart but without time to return to his lane. With sudden death approaching, Jump-Start farted, wet his pants, and steered his vehicle away from danger with the little strength he had left. The only words he said were, 'Mi dead now.' People nearby saw the violent crash of the runaway truck into Jump-Start's truck. Even people miles away could hear the crash. The onlookers unanimously shouted, 'A fi you fault' to the runaway driver. I'm not sure if that driver survived, but Jah was right there to snatch our beloved brother from death's jaws with only a broken leg. Thank God he has healed well and got some insurance money for personal injuries. He didn't get much for the truck, but since we all benefited from its services, I didn't hear anyone grumble when we decided to make a down payment on a replacement truck with our collected resources and registered it in Jump-Start's name. With continued success in our agricultural program, we will pay for that truck in due time. I thank you for accepting my invitation to settle in this place. Thanks also for your contribution to the experiment. Now that you have heard from me, what do each of you have to say for yourself and to the rest of us about this New Canaan experience?"

Dunce-Man was the first to speak. "Thanks be to Jah for saving Jump-Start. One love brother! I share the joys of our three years accomplishment. But I look forward to the greater joy of us owning this place after we occupied it for seven years. Yes, brethren, I'm looking toward the time when we are no longer squatters, but owners of this precious land. I hope you all know that under current laws, squatters who occupy vacant land for at least seven years continuously, can file a legitimate claim for the parcel of land and receive a valid title from the government. We need to start planning the takeover. Preliminary preparations include a smart lawyer to represent rather than subvert our interest. We will need a land surveyor to establish the property's boundaries and register his map of the area with the Survey Department, before we can get the title. All twelve of our names could be on one title, or we could subdivide the land into twelve lots, then have twelve separate titles for each of us. Meanwhile, pray without ceasing that by then, the ruling powers will not change current laws in ways that negatively alter current laws and completely deprive us of our hard-earned fortune."

Many brethren did not know about those laws mentioned by Dunce-Man. But the prospect of owning a piece of land as a birthright from Jah the Father to his lost children brought a mixture of tears and laughter from the brethren. With those mixed emotions, some spontaneously shouted, "Four more years! Four more years!"

But other brethren were ambivalent about whether future title of the property should be jointly owned or subdivided into individual holdings. Stick-Man expressed the following concerns. "In earlier discussions we talked about how envy operates. It is not content with admiring a desirable object. It's intent on depriving the owner of the envied object. So, if we subdivide the land and distribute it with existing cultivation, some people will get coffee fields, some with will get ganga fields, while others get woodland to cut down trees and burn coal. There will be huge disparity in the work required by each group to earn their living. Envy will not take that disparity lying down."

Harry intervened by explaining various types of ownership. "I learned something in economics that will help us deal with Stick-Man's concerns. There are three types of ownerships;—sole ownership, partnership, and corporation. Currently, we don't fit into any of these categories because we have no legal status to the land we occupy. Let's say Stick-Man is the backra man and sole owner of this property, he is responsible for all its incomes and losses. His ownership dies at his death. The second type of ownership is a partnership. In that case Stick-Man and several other people jointly own this property. They share the proceeds and the debts equally. The partnership ends when the last living partner dies. The third type of ownership is corporate. It's the most complex of the three. It is not tied to living people. It is a separate entity that acts as stand-in for real people. Its owners use the corporation to borrow money from banks and anywhere possible. They pay themselves from the profit, while exploring opportunities to grow the corporation. If the corporation is not successful, people blame the stand-in, rather than humans. Unlike sole ownership and partnership, corporate ownership can survive the deaths of its partners. It seems to me that we have been operating as an informal partnership and the fact that we accomplished so much in such a short time proves that unity is strength. But let's not forget that we own nothing. If the government reclaims the land tomorrow, we would have lost all our invested labor in this place. So, don't allow daydreams to interfere with reality. Individual ownership of a little piece of land will not make us competitive against the backra men with thousands of acres. It will leave us among those people who are sleep walking in Coronation Market. Our way forward requires us to practice addition, rather than subtraction."

Stick-Man responded, "If I heard you correctly, our best option is joint ownership. After we own the land, we have a responsibility to make it as productive as possible with help of family members, friends, and even strangers who share our interest. Meanwhile, everybody continues to get money from ganga, coffee, coal, and everything that this land produces. But you mentioned another important factor. How do we prolong the life of this operation after we die? How do we start the next generation at a higher level than scratch?"

Dunce-Man chimed in happily. "I thank Harry for underscoring the importance of owning this land as a big step forward in our development. Joint ownership reinforces what we have been doing. Unity is strength. I like the idea of thinking big, while our feet are on the ground."

Stick-Man spoke next, saying, "I'm proud of our accomplishments together and grateful for the personal benefits that I received. Before I changed my ways, I was one of the slickest pickpockets in Kingston. I earned the name Stick-Man, from those who were amazed by my dexterity with a stick. I practiced various tricks with sticks that after a time, my arms, my hands, and my fingers could manipulate a target like a finely tuned instrument. I distracted people with the stick in either hand, while the free hand claimed the desired prizes from pockets, pouches, and purses. I could also run like a sprinter to escape the wrath of my victims. Although my speed had never been officially timed, I have no doubt that I would have been successful against current olympians in the one-hundred-yard flat race or hurdle. Back then when I was unsure where I would get the next penny, I saved a little cash each day in the post office, buying books of penny stamps. I continued the habit of saving for the unpredictable rainy day. But now that I can save a little more, I put most in Barclay's Bank and less in the post office. Those are the safest places I know to save money. They even pay me something called interest to keep the money safe in their bank. Can you believe that them pay me fi keep my money safe? So, for everyone of you who still hides your money under a mattress, this message is for you. It's time to change your ways of sleeping on your money. Wake up to modern times of saving your extra cash in Barclay's Bank, to keep it safe and growing."

After Stick-Man's comments, the reactions on some men's faces betrayed their guilt of unsafely storing hidden treasures under their mattresses. Even their later urgent need to catch a ride with Jump-

Start on his next trip to a bank in Yallahs or Kingston indicated they were banking the old fashion way, unsafely, under their mattresses.

Harry had the last words and began his closing remarks of the session, saying to the men, "Please join me in a shoutout to our visionary leaders, Ras Joshua, and Barracuda."

In response, the men stood and shouted, "Big up Rastafari and his disciples, Joshua and Barracuda, who captured New Canaan without arms, but with the blessings of the Most-High."

Harry continued with his remarks, saying, "Three years in New Canaan has changed the trajectory of my life. I overcame the awful experience of being an orphan, to be the son of a mother and father, who are slowly climbing their economic ladders, while living in England. I am no longer naked, starving, restless, despised, and teetering on the verge of insanity. Thanks to Jah's rescue team, who humorously addressed me as brother Zacchaeus when they saw me climbing down from my perch in the tree on Darling Street. With their guidance and help, I am doing more than pick up crumbs of learning, by eavesdropping on random discussions among university students in the park or the market. In the next year after Hopton and I pass two more subjects, we will be eligible for university studies here in Jamaica, or overseas in England, Canada, and America. The whole world of knowledge has been open to us. England strongly beckons me to get the education while reconnecting with my mother and get acquainted with my father. But I don't want my personal need for strong ties with my parents to distract from my mission of breaking and extracting slave chains that remain as impediments to Black people's progress. Slave mentality rather than true knowledge, is directly responsible for the deprivation of Adam's Black children who sleep uncomfortably in Coronation Markets located all over the world. The echoes of Barracuda's reprimand still ring in my ears, saying, 'Nowhere is not a place to live.' Do you remember that statement David/Barracuda? I will never forget those words until I die. I remember your words when I encounter people who have been stripped of their hopes for a better life. They walk without going anywhere. They talk to themselves, but no one else. They seldom look up, but always looking down, in hopes of finding discarded scraps of food and trinkets, although they had nowhere to store them. I want to grow up to be farsighted and caring as both of you, but I worry sometimes that higher studies will distract me from the realities of people in the lower levels of society, because the economic and political theories I have been exposed to, teach students how to optimize resources and power, but not much about resolving the problems caused by diminished access to both.

"Thankfully, there are many examples of people, like Marcus Garvey, Alexander Bustamante, and Norman Manley who were resourceful in using their wider knowledge of the world to solve some of the local problems here in Jamaica. Their efforts resulted in various improvements for people, most noticeably those in the labor market. The improvements included higher wages, but shorter work week at a cost to plantation owners. I am also encouraged by stories of African leaders, Kwame Nkrumah of Africa's Gold Coast, Jomo Kenyatta of Kenya, and Julius Nyerere of Tanzanian who studied overseas and returned home to apply their newly acquired knowledge to the solutions of local problems. Surprisingly, some people who were potential beneficiaries of their efforts to break the chains of slavery, resisted their intervention vigorously and sometimes successfully.

Finally, the lessons I learned from our living together, remain useful models that I will preserve and share. No doubt each of us has his favorite lesson, but I hope your favorite will include those taught by our good friends, Jump-Start and Barracuda. Who can forget these memorable words by Jump-Start, that wiped the grin off our faces? 'Always have a secondary source of power to boost your battery in case you need to jump start your engine.' Or those by Barracuda, 'Jah is our source of power and with his support we will be always good to go.' But what does good to go mean to you? before we go anywhere, we must wake up and chart our course. Wake up, brethren! No time to be sleepwalking on market floors in Jamaica, Africa, and everywhere in the world. May blessings precede and sustain us and succeeding generations, all the days of our lives. One love!"

Joshua and Barracuda remained quiet during the discussions, but everyone else could see that they were pleased with Harry's continuing positive display of his knowledge. During the three years since they met Harry, they have been contemplating how to satisfy his longing to reunite with his mother and meet his father. Harry's decision to continue his education in England rather than America will be influenced by that longing. They started planning to celebratethat reunion right there in New Canaan.

CHAPTER 11

Reunion

Echoes of four more years were heard beyond the boundaries of New Canaan. But the anticipated reality of owning fertile land in New Canaan was not celebrated by everyone in Gap. Science-Man's distinguished career in that community had peaked and he was no closer to discovering the elixir that could make people more humane. He was little more than an observer of the spectacular development in New Canaan, under the leadership of previously despised Rasta men. The women he recruited to work on the Rasta farm were spreading positive stories about the Rasta men. Mary told a friend, "I used to hear that Rasta men disrespect women, but I can speak for myself and four other women who work for them bagging coal, we get nuff respect."

But even more irritating to Science-Man, the women hung around the Rasta men after work, listening to their reasoning sessions, eating their Ital food, before returning to Gap spewing Rasta doctrines that a Black man in Africa is a living god. He grew up singing the hymn "Onward Christian Soldier," and he felt justified in taking up arms against the heretics. He started by conducting religious meetings on Sundays and Wednesday evenings. His main theme was Judas betraying Jesus. "Brothers and sisters, hear the word of the Lord. In the last days, Satan will use false prophets to turn your hearts from righteousness to wickedness. In the same way that Judas sold Jesus for thirty pieces of silver, we have our neighbors in New Canaan selling not only Jesus, but God, for a few acres of land. They blaspheme God's holy name by declaring that God is a living Black man, rather than the divine supreme ruler of our lives and the entire universe. Their idol worship is preparing them for hell. Do you want to join them in that everlasting fire? Who is on the Lord side? Raise your hand?"

When Science-Man's questions did not get the enthusiastic response he anticipated from the few people gathered at the service, he used other strategies to dissuade them from working in New Canaan. The medicines he prescribed were prolonging people's illnesses rather than making them well. Their poultry and livestock were dying of mysterious sickness, presumably because God was turning His back on them for failing to repent from sinful association with infidels. One night, he wore a disguise and sneaked into a neighbor's back-yard to leave telltale signs of God's displeasure. He did not see their sleeping dog at the kitchen door. His unfamiliar presence startled the dog. But unlike humans who might have run away from the ghostly image, the dog knew nothing about ghosts. It woke up to an unfa-miliar image that should not be in the yard. It instinctively began barking loudly at the ghostly intruder. Science-Man retreated, turned around and ran away from the dog and the possibility of being iden-tified by the neighbor. But the dog was in close pursuit and attacked him. Science-Man had a dilemma. He had to avoid being seriously injured by the dog and he had to get away from the neighbor's yard before being discovered as the intruder. He didn't like the option of losing control of the situation by running with his back to the dog. He decided to walk backward and use his flailing arms to combat the dog. But each backward step in the dark was more perilous than the previous step. His problem was compounded by the fact that the dog was black and almost invisible, except for its terrifying shining eyes.

The dog bit Science-Man's leg when it grabbed his trousers. Science-Man screamed in a high-pitched sound to disguise his voice. He fell to the ground and spilled the chicken parts he was planning to leave as bad omens in the neighbor's kitchen. The dog immediately lost interest in him and went for the chicken parts. Although Science-Man got home without further injury, he left blood stains along the way and a piece of his trousers as forensic evidence.

Concerned that his activities were not disruptive enough to discourage Gap residents from accepting employment in New Canaan, Science-Man eventually felt enough rage to confront the Rasta men on their turf in New Canaan. He recruited a dozen men armed with their Bibles to accompany him.

The brethren in New Canaan had finished the day's work, eaten their dinner, and preparing for the evening's reasoning session, when Science-Man and his supporters arrived.

Joshua greeted them by asking, "Wha a guan? You come to join our reasoning session?"

"Not really," Science-Man replied. "God sent us with the Christian message to lighten your path. It is written, 'They that walk-in darkness shall see the light. We also want to instruct you in how to give back to the Lord through his anointed representative.'"

Joshua responded, "We have the light and I'm sure our light is brighter than yours. It would be wasting both our time to prove whose light is brighter. So, let me deal with the second issue. Who is the Lord's representative? How much do I give?"

Science-Man said, "I'm the Lord's representative in this part of the island. I have been ordained as a local elder in the Church of God. The Lord said in the book of Malachi, 'Bring ye all the tithes into the storehouse and I will open the windows of heaven and pour out blessings that you will not have room enough to receive it.'"

Joshua asked, "How does your storehouse look right now? Is it overflowing with blessings that your poor neighbors have been putting in your storehouse? How does God get your tithe? I understand from your neighbors that your hands are too soft to work the land. That's why you have been a science man, playing abracadabra with bushes like a magician. Compared to other people in this part of Jamaica, your hands are soft, because you have always reaped where you have not sewn. You come straight out of the Whiteman's play book, begging on behalf of your invisible God. Unlike you, we brethren embrace the blessings of working the land for ourselves and not for the backra man. We have defied the label of being stupid and lazy. My hope is that you would learn something from our example. No wonder old people used to say, 'You can take donkey to the river, but you can't force him to drink.'"

Harry joined the conversation by saying, "My mother's grandfather used to say, 'You are either with us or against us.' Your demands strongly indicate that you are against us. You have been drinking too much of your medicine and it has damaged your brains. You missed the big picture of what we brethren are accomplishing in New Canaan. We are breaking the chains of slavery that white people embedded in Black people's brains. We are reclaiming our independence. White people know that unity is strength, if they can get us to fight each other, they win. When our African fathers sold us into slavery, white people won. They continue to win when mental slavery keeps us ignorant and divided. In your eyes, you might be the wisest man in Gap. You might know something about bush medicine, but you are not a scientist. Your work does not improve people's health. In the end, you are not rich. You are still a slave, but you can't see your chains. So, listen up. Our sources told us that you are an undercover informant to the slave masters. This is not a true or false issue, because you can't own up to who you are before your church brothers. You betray people who trust you with their personal problems by making many of them worse than before they sought your help. But you come here with your Bible like you are a saint. Everybody in Gap will soon know what some of them already know about you."

One of the men who accompanied Science-Man to the meeting said, "I have known this man all my life and your description of him does not sound like the person I know. It's true that his hands are more delicate than most of our hands, but that is not the same thing as being underhanded."

The old Kingston fighting spirit filled some of the brethren with rage while they were listening. Some started to sharpen their machetes. A few of them grabbed Science-Man and ripped off his shirt. Others tied his hands behind him and shouted, "Burn him! Burn him up in the coal pit." One man with a machete rushed forward shouting, "Burning is a painful death, but it takes too long to kill a pig like this. I can do it instantly. It's just like chopping off a hog's head. I don't mind going to prison for killing this pig."

Barracuda, with the help of other men, restrained the man with the machete, while Science-Man lost control of his bladder, wet his pants, before feebly defending himself. "Brethren, I came in peace. You know that I have demonstrated my support of your business by recruiting excellent workers and recommending them to you. But as a Christian, God appointed me to bring you into His fold and teach you principles of gratitude to Him through His anointed representative here on earth. I did what any anointed person would do, I presented the truth to you."

Harry interrupted him, "You have had grievance against us for a long time, even before you started to recruit workers for us. Your efforts to turn people against us included sermons describing us as false prophets. You harass people with obeah tricks to discourage them from working for us. You sprinkled ashes at their front door, hung John Crow feathers on their back door, and left one and sometimes two chicken heads in their kitchens as warning signs. You have done too much. You don't fit into Jah's plan of uniting people. The brethren and I will present the real you to Gap people. We will tell them about your obeah tricks and the negative things you have done to threaten their health and their livelihood. We will work with them to drive you out of the district immediately. You are dismissed! We are finished with you!"

Turning to Joshua, Harry asked, "Do you think it's time for a revival in Gap like those you used to conduct at Parade? We can gather a crowd with the people who work for us and those that Dunce-Man know."

Joshua agreed by saying, "Consider it done."

Science-Man was still wet and tied up in knots literally and figuratively, when his friends escorted him from the Brethren's premises. The closer he got to his village the more his heart pounded with fear that his companions would spread bad news about his humiliation by some Rasta men. Eventually his heart was pounding for a different reason. He was concerned about the thick smoke and fire he saw in the section of the district where he lived. His pace quickened. He arrived in the district to the sad discovery that his house was on fire. He saw spectators and heard them praying that the fire does not spread to their houses. There was no running water nor firefighters to put out the blaze and no concern about his plight. After the flames, he experienced the crumbling of his life. He lost all his possessions and could not even change the clothes he soiled during the traumatic encounter with the brethren. Rather than offering him shelter, his neighbors shunned him, when they heard rumors that he was responsible for the macabre discoveries in and around their homes. That night Science-Man started a new journey into homelessness and despair, but with less confidence in God and his obeah tricks.

After Science-Man left, Joshua and Barracuda revived talks about the surprise party for Harry and men in the Science Club. "When will be the best time to have this event and who should be invited?" Barracuda asked.

Joshua smiled and said, "I want it to be a real surprise party. So, here's the plan. You persuade Victor to return to Jamaica for a visit. You will meet him in Portland to the surprise of his parents and yours. At the end of the Portland visit, both sets of parents will join you and Victor on a trip to New Canaan. While you are working on Victor, I will have Lucy working on Virginia to return to Plantation Village for a visit at the same time. Lucy will persuade Virginia with the argument that she deserves a sunny break from England's cold weather and people at home will be glad to see her. It's best if Lucy meets Virginia at the pier in Kingston or at the airport, take her to the Plantation Village, have a mini reunion with Tarta, before coming to New Canaan. You and Victor will arrive at New Canaan in the evening of July 31st. Virginia will arrive with Tarta and Lucy the morning of August 1st, Emancipation Day. Harry corresponds regularly with Virginia, but Lucy will advise her to keep her planned visit a secret from him. Although he corresponds less frequently with his dad, you must tell Victor not to inform Harry about his planned visit, because we want it to be a surprise."

"Great idea. Harry will have passed his next set of high school subjects and may have been accepted to universities in the US and Britain. When do we begin?" Barracuda asked.

"Now," responded Joshua.

After speaking with Barracuda about the plan, Joshua remembered that both Victor and Virginia entered England illegally. As a stowaway, Victor may not have a passport or valid identification to obtain a new one. "Barracuda, remember that Victor may need help to get travel documents. Ask him if he can travel overseas or if he needs your help to get Jamaican birth certificate or other identifying information to speed up the processing of travel documents. In Virginia's case, her travel documents are false. But she also could right that problem by speaking to British lawyers who know how to fix such problems for people from Europe. I will tell Lucy to follow up on that issue. Hopefully Virginia will return home with her true identity and not the one she has been living with England."

Joshua's tasks were more complicated, because he had to work through a third party, Lucy, whom he didn't know well. But both he and Barracuda accepted their challenges by saying to each other, "On your mark! Get set! Go!"

Victor was happy to receive the invitation. Two months later he responded, "No problem with travel documents. When my employers needed to send me with a crew to work on a project in Spain, they helped me fix my immigration problems. The stumbling block is getting time off from work. This company has specific vacation period for each employee and late July, early August is not my vacation time. I will do my best to negotiate the time off, but if my other strategies fail, I may ask you to send me a medical report in July, stating that my parents are gravely ill."

Lucy reported that Virginia was excited about returning to Jamaica to see her son and Tarta. Her letter stated, "I successfully finished my basic nursing training and I plan to do midwifery in the fall. A Nigerian Lawyer helped me to correct my identity and my immigration documents are currently being updated. I'm happy to be using my right name again. The foreseeable problem is not being able to pay for my return passage to England and finish my training.

A one-way ticket to Jamaica is not in the long-term best interest of my family. But to be restrained by financial circumstances from seeing my son, will likely break my heart. What a dilemma."

Tears welled up in Joshua's eyes, then cascaded over his mustache onto his beard. In his thoughts, "No woman should suffer that much pain." He wiped the tears, thought of a possible solution and its accompanying complication. "Why not ask Victor for the money to pay her travel expenses? After all he is indebted to her for taking care of their son for most of the boy's life without Victor's support. But here's the problem. How does Barracuda and I convince victor to give us that much money without telling him that Virginia needs it?"

Barracuda suggested an alternative. "Let's send her the money upfront, and after the reunion we inform Victor that we paid her passage. I believe he will man up and pay us back. But even if he does not repay us, the reunion of Virginia and her son will be worth every penny we spent on her trip."

Joshua responded, "Two heads are better than one."

Joshua sent the money via Lucy to Virginia and received confirmation several weeks later, that Virginia was booked on a flight to Kingston on July 27th. She will return August 3rd, two days before resuming her studies.

It was now time to prepare the brethren for the event, while keeping Harry in the dark. A week before the grand event, Joshua gave Harry a special assignment in the presence of Barracuda. "Harry, we have a special job for you. We would like you to persuade Tarta and Lucy to join us in celebrating Emancipation Day, August 1st. Tarta can share your room. Lucy will sleep in one of the guest rooms. Tell her to bring her daughter with her."

"When do I go?"

"You can leave tomorrow, so that Tarta will have enough lead time to prepare for the visit."

After Harry left on July 27, Joshua called a meeting of the brethren about the upcoming celebration. "Listen up everybody, we have a ring ding celebration on Emancipation Day next week. We will have special guests, including Harry's and Barracuda's relatives.

If everything goes according to plan, we will continue to honor one another's families each year on Emancipation Day. Is that okay?"

"Speaking for myself, nothing is wrong with that plan. But what do other men think?" said Stick-Man.

Hopeton responded, "Celebrating our freedom with our families is consistent with our liberation struggle. It's breaking the mental chains that bar us from family whom we need to love but bind us to our oppressors."

"Well," said Joshua, "we must have a jamboree with lots of food and music. Who will oversee the food? Who will take charge of the music?"

"If is music unno want, just talk, because is music unno wi get. I will take charge of di music and play nuff One Drop Riddim fi lively up di place," said Quiet-Man.

Dunce-Man volunteered to be the head cook by saying, "Any worthwhile celebration must have nuff food. The menu will include boiled and roasted food such as bammy, ital stew, and escovitche fish. Some people's palate may prefer fish than the ital stew, so they will have a choice. We will wash down the food with jelly coconut water and lemonade. Then polish off the meal with a desert of jackfruit and star apple. I will try to get watermelon also. Unno, look how much spit a drain outa Stick-Man mout even before mi start cook di food. Learn fi control yourself, man!"

Joint laughter from everyone indicated that they approved the plans.

Meanwhile, Harry's surprise visit with Tarta was going well. Tarta was happy to see his great-grandson and welcomed the opportunity to see what Harry and his Rasta brethren were doing in the land of New Canaan. But Harry could not find Lucy, who was in a secret hiding place, until she arrived with Virginia. She showed up about two hours after Harry arrived. "Good evening, Tarta!"

"Oh, Harry! What are you doing here?"

Virginia was hiding behind the house, in a disguise she wore from the airport to prevent people at Bulla Shop from recognizing and following her home as they did on Harry's first return to the district.

"Close your eyes. No peeping and turn your back to me. I have a surprise for you. You can open your eyes after I count to fifteen." Virginia could hear Lucy counting and quietly walked into the house. She stood behind Lucy. "Now turn around. Open your eyes."

They did not recognize the woman they saw standing beside Lucy. She was plump, especially around the hips. Strangely, she began taking off several skirts that covered the slacks she was wearing. Lucy unzipped one blouse from behind, but there were others that she and the woman were unbuttoning in the front. After the skirts and blouses were removed, a grey-haired woman with wrinkled skin on her face stood beside Lucy. But they were too shocked by the unusual incident to process what was happening. Eventually, Tarta said to Lucy, "Where did you get this obeah woman that you bring to my house?"

Lucy responded, "This is a good obeah woman. It's time you have good luck."

After that remark by Lucy, the woman took off the wig to reveal her natural black hair. Then Lucy said, "Please close your eyes briefly again before greeting this special woman." Lucy assisted Virginia in removing the face mask and said, "Abracadabra! Open sesame! You may open your eyes now."

Tarta and Harry saw a woman sweating profusely from the combination of the tropical heat and the extra clothing to disguise her identity, but she was unmistakably Virginia. She broke the shocked silence. "Good evening, Tarta and my darling son Harry. I am very, very happy to be with you."

With humor in his voice, Tarta addressed Lucy, "Are you sure this is Virginia and not an obeah woman?" Everyone smiled, but Harry had a lump in his throat that choked the words he wanted to say to his mom. He rushed to her, embraced her firmly, then rested his tear-stained face on her shoulder.

Virginia started a lament. "I pinched myself when I arrived in Kingston this afternoon. I thanked God for taking care of both of you during my absence. I had good intentions of going to England and earning money to support both of you better than when I was a higgler woman in Jamaica. But my plans had to be adjusted to fit the reality of surviving in a foreign country without even a friend. I wept day and night when I did not receive responses to my letters about you. I was sure that you would not abandon me because I was out of sight. So, I thought something went terribly wrong with both of you at the same time. I even felt worse when I did not hear from Lucy. I wept night and day in my solitude. I worried when I learned that Harry became a Rasta man, because I thought that his appearance and ideas would be an unnecessary setback in modern society. But I'm hopeful that his decision to pursue formal education will eventually give him an enlightened view of the world, not only of Jamaica."

Tarta joined Harry in giving Virginia a welcome embrace before saying, "At long last I can answer questions about you and put to rest the speculations about your disappearance and death. You and Harry are among the few people who left Plantation Village and lived a better life than we who remained. The more I think about that, the more I realize the goodness of God. I have met Harry's Rasta friends and they are reinforcing in his head the need to break the invisible chains of mental slavery that remains embedded in Black people's brains. When you have a chance to speak with him about his beliefs, you will discover that your son is on his way to becoming an inspiring leader like Paul Bogle or Marcus Garvey."

"Time out!" said Lucy. "Anybody hungry? Let's continue the conversation over dinner. It will be more convenient to eat the food I prepared for this occasion at my house."

Tarta, Harry, and Lucy used their bodies as shields in the twilight, as they escorted Virginia to Lucy's house. After the meal they returned to Tarta's house unnoticed. Virginia had a good night sleep and could hardly wait for daybreak to go with Lucy for an early morning swim.

On her way from the beach she said hello to Bulla Watson, who at first, refused to believe his eyes. "You returned as quietly as you left, and you look like God has been blessing you. Have you returned to stay? Or will you be leaving again?"

"Everything is in God's hand. He will decide," Virginia responded. She gave the same answer to similar questions from the people she visited and encountered during the next four days leading to the Emancipation Day celebration in New Canaan.

Meanwhile, Victor, the other surprise visitor from England, was granted leave from his job without the help of emergency health notices about his parents. He arrived in Port Antonio on July 29 with plans to join the Emancipation celebration on August 1. He had a wonderful reunion with his parents, siblings, and old friends. most importantly, he and Peter/Barracuda, had fun reliving their past, but Barracuda wanted to know about Victor's plans and learned the following. "I'm studying to become an electrical engineer. After a couple of years knocking about in London, I got a job in a radio outfit and was fascinated to learn how unseen electricity can be used like an instrument to manipulate things. With curiosity running high, I registered in a technical college and took courses offered by City and Guilds to make me an electrical engineer. The studies keep me busy and mostly out of trouble. With the help of Jah, I will earn the professional diploma in three years. I worried about Harry all the time and wondered if he would ever want to have anything to do with me. We have exchanged a few letters and I love what's on his mind. He is serious about getting all of us out of the invisible grasp of slavery. Every time I read one of his letters, he reinforces my determination to press ahead with my training. I hope I'll be able to bond with him before I return to London."

"Did you ever inquire about Virginia or see her in London? I'm not trying to get into your business, but I'm curious," Barracuda inquired.

"Truthfully, I never stopped thinking about her. But what would I say to her after the trouble I put her through. She was one of the smartest young people in the district. Her future was uncertain, because of structural impediments of the plantation system. But of everyone there, she was most likely to succeed. I know in my heart that I had no bad intentions toward her. In fact, my pet name for her was dawta. With her pregnancy and the birth of Harry, I Instinctively became Harry's grandpa, and his dad. I avoided a possible blood bath in the district when I left, but Virginia was stuck. She had to cope with a daily diet of venom spewed by gossiping neighbors, while enduring the pressures of raising a son without predictable support from his father or anyone else. She forged her own way out. To answer your questions more directly, I have not seen Victoria, but I have always wished her well."

Victor, Barracuda, and their parents arrived in New Canaan the evening of July 31. They were warmly greeted by the brethren. But Victor kept waiting for the opportunity to greet Harry. When he discovered that Harry was not among the greeters, his disappointment prompted him to ask Joshua. "Do you think Harry is avoiding me? He has not come to say hello to me or his grandparents."

Joshua tried to relieve him of his disappointment. "Harry is not here. He is on assignment to bring Tarta and Lucy to the celebration tomorrow morning. He will be surprised to see you, because we did not tell him that you are expected. So, you have extra time to think about what you will say to him. How do your parents feel about hanging out with Rasta men? Given the hardworking person your dad is, how does he feel about our work to increase productivity of this land?"

"Daddy's unspoken complement is the fact that he has not said anything negative to me about you guys."

After everyone else settled down for the night, Joshua, Barracuda, and Victor shared weed in a chillum pipe while reflecting on their unpredictable journeys that brought them together again. Victor articulated their quiet reflection when he said, "I give thanks for this opportunity to be reunited with both of you in this place that you have inherited from Jah. It is reassuring to know that the will of the Almighty is being done on earth, not in an imaginary heaven."

August 1 began with a beautiful sunrise and gentle breeze. Quiet-Man took early advantage of nature's gift to set up the sound system. He attached wires to speakers in the meeting house and at several locations on the compound. He built a small platform to set up the sound system, but he would wait for everyone to be awake, before testing the system.

Dunce-Man also started his preparation early. His activities were less obvious, but easily recognized by the distinctive smell of spices he was using to marinate the food. But hidden from sight and smell, was Joshua's overall activities, to ensure success of the event; while achieving peace, if not reconciliation, between Victor and Virginia, who will be seeing each other for the first time since she became pregnant with Harry.

At 10:00 AM, Harry's arrival was imminent. The brethren continued to add finishing touches to the preparation. They unfurled two flags and hoisted them at entrance to the meeting house. On the left, was Garvey's Pan African flag with three horizontal bands of red, black, and green in descending order. On the right, the Ethiopian horizontal tri-color flag with green, yellow, and red in descending order. The symbol of the Conquering Lion of Judah prominently displayed on the yellow panel. Victor's mom and Barracuda's mom huddled together under a tree, laughing hysterically. Their husbands under another tree were sharing opinions about the brethren's adventure. Mr. Amos, Victor's dad, said to Mr. Jones, "These Rasta men are different from those we see in Portland. They work like regular people, the way we train our boys, when they were growing up. But few regular people would do what they have done to unite Victor with Harry. This reunion is worth celebrating."

At Joshua's signal, everyone shouted the congratulatory cheer. "Harry is back. Hip! Hip! Hurray! Hip! Hip! Hurrah!"

Harry joyfully introduced his accompanying visitors by saying, "Listen up everybody, this is my mother Virginia, my great-grandfather Tarta, and my mother's best friend Lucy. My mom dropped in from England on a surprise visit while I was in Plantation Village. That's right. But I don't think that's why you are chuckling. My guess is that the coincidence of her arrival while I was visiting Tarta was more surprising to me than it is to those of you who planned the visit and kept it secret. But I will be forever grateful to you for breathing new life into Tarta, for rekindling mom's and Lucy's friendship, and for satisfying my dreams of experiencing my mother's love."

After Harry's remarks there was an interlude of music, while the brethren and visitors greeted the newest arrivals. Then Harry saw his look alike and thought someone was wearing a mask. Harry approached him and said, "Why are you wearing a mask, this is not a John Canoe celebration, it's Emancipation Day."

The voice responded, "I'm not wearing a mask today. Touch my face."

As Harry reached out to touch the man's face, Victor embraced him and said, "I am Victor, your dad. I arrived a few days ago in Portland. Joshua sent Barracuda to escort my parents, his parents, and me to this emancipation celebration. They did not tell me that Virginia would be here, and I have no idea if she knows I'm here. Victor and Barracuda went all out to make this a very memorable day for you. I hope my presence won't dilute your positive experiences. I would like to formally present you to Mom and Dad, when you feel up to it. You have triumphed over tremendous odds without my support, but Jah granted me a second chance and I intend to do much more than apologize for the past. I will do what's right, if you will let me."

Harry pulled away as his mind flashed back on Victor's treatment of Virginia, and the dirty remarks he heard about Victor from Virginia's friends and Tarta. "He smoked weed, played dominoes, and disappeared. He is unreliable." But he also remembered Barracuda's positive stories about Victor. He was trying to balance those competing impressions against the real person in his presence.

"What do I call you?" Harry asked

"It's your choice. Call me a name or a title, whatever makes you comfortable."

"I'll think about it. Incidentally, your mask fits you well. It gives me an idea what to expect in the coming years."

Joshua assembled the group in the meeting room with Tarta standing at his right and members of the Knowledge Club standing at his left. "Tarta I thank you for inspiring Harry to break the chains of mental slavery embedded in Black people's brains. After he relayed your inspiration to the brethren, we realized that knowledge is the master key to unlock invisible slave chains in our heads. Stated another way, white people's most successful weapon against us is their knowledge. With that awareness, these brethren organized a Knowledge Club to support formal education through correspondence courses. To date, Harry and Hopeton have each passed eight GCE subjects to satisfy university entrance requirements in Great

Britain and the US. Hopeton plans to become a scientist, Harry plans to be an economist. With Jah's blessing they will return to Jamaica to make revolutionary changes in Black people's lives. Other members of the Knowledge Club, including Stick-Man, Dunce-Man, and Jump-Start have also passed several GCE subjects. Three cheers for the Knowledge Club members."

While celebrating the achievements of brethren in the Knowledge Club, Joshua reminded everyone that current achievements in their community of New Canaan, benefited from everyone's contribution. "Everyone accepts formal education as one dimension of development. We acknowledge that it helps us build more quickly on the foundations that others have started. But when all is said and done, our success is rooted in the wise use of our collective experiences. During today's celebration, I hope our visiting friends will feel at home with us. Let's eat, drink, and have a good time."

Joshua then led a chant, "What do we want?"

"Freedom!"

"When do we want it?"

"Now!"

"Hip-hip-hurrah! Hip-hip-hurrah! Hip-hip-hurrah!"

After the cheers, Quiet-Man started playing music signaling time to eat. The brethren serving the meal asked the visitors to find comfortable seats, outdoor under shade trees. Instinctively, visitors who knew one another sat together. It was evident among people from Portland, St. Thomas, and those from Gap. The spontaneous laughter, the request for additional food and drinks, confirmed that everyone was having a good time. The good feeling was constantly reinforced with the syncopating rhythm of the music. Some people who couldn't decide whether to eat or to dance, did both. They grooved off-beat to the syncopation of the music with their plate of food as a partner.

Later, Harry escorted his mother to meet Victor's parents. Ms. Ruth spoke first, "I apologize for the way Victor treated you and for the hardships you and Harry experienced. Me and his father raise our children right, but we have no control over their decisions when they are adults. Victor chose his own path and we lost him for a long time, but thank God this event brought him back home. He admitted the wrong he did to you and Harry and asked us to open our hearts to both of you."

Virginia responded, "Harry told me how gracious you, Mr. Amos, and Victor's siblings were to him when he visited you. I'm grateful for your kindness. But I was the Humpty Dumpty in Plantation Village that had the great fall at fifteen years old. That fall shattered me in ways that no king's man nor any man can put this Humpty Dumpty together again. I don't blame you for your adult son's behavior. I hate him for abandoning me, to ridicule and the prolonged feeling of helplessly falling off a cliff. The straws I grasped on my perilous decent gave way. I landed with a thud in Coronation Market as a higgler, while your son turned his back on me and his son. Ironically, we would not be here today celebrating Harry's achievements, had it not been for his unlikely encounter with Victor's friends, Joshua and Barracuda. I have learned important lessons from such unpredictable experiences, that I should never judge a book by its cover. Despite those lessons, I have two fervent hopes. Number one, that Harry's physical resemblance to his father remains skin-deep. Number two, that Harry will chose a better role model than Victor."

Mr. Amos acknowledged Victor's disappointing behavior but expressed the wish that links between his family and Virginia's family, especially Harry, would not be broken. "I met Harry once and I just met you. I join Ruth in apologizing for Victor's behavior, which we knew nothing about. While I can't undo the past, I will do my best to preserve the link between Harry and this family. We love you Harry, and we are sorry for the bad experiences you and your mom suffered because of Victor."

After visiting Victor's parents, Harry accompanied Virginia on her visit with Barracuda's parents to thank them for their son's friendship of Harry. Her final gratitude was reserved for Joshua and Barracuda. "No mother has a better heart than you, gentlemen. Your kindness to my son reminds me of the Good Samaritan in the Bible. Rather than turning away from my emotionally wounded son, as so many in Coronation Market had done, you embraced him, you clothed him, you housed him, and you fed him. You even listened to his yearnings to fulfill Tarta's wish, that he be the person to break Black people's mental chains of slavery. You did not dismiss his idea as absurd. You nourished the idea and supported his efforts to acquire knowledge as a key element in the endeavor. You included him in your creation of this community's cooperative wealth building incubator. As if that were not enough, you engineered this celebration where Harry could meet his father and be reunited with me. I was not happy when I discovered that Harry became a Rasta like his father. Thankfully, while I was inclined to focus on outward appearances, God redirected my attention to view the works of your hearts. Thanks for all you have done for my son and me. I hope you will continue to be rewarded with his success."

Shortly after the reunion, Virginia returned to England without interacting with Harry's father. She allowed Victor to fade as the dimly lit background, against the enlightened images of her son Harry's accomplishments.

REFERENCES

Leonard E. Barrett, Sr., The Rastafarians, Beacon Press, Boston Mass. 1977

Barry Chavannes, Rastafari, Roots and Ideology, Syracuse Press, 1994

Robert A Hill, Editor; Barbara Bair, Associate Editor, Marcus Garvey Life Lessons, University of California Press, LA, 1987

Michael Manley, A Voice At the Workplace, Reflections on Colonialism and the Jamaican Worker, Howard University Press, Washington D.C. 1991

Richard Price, Editor, Maroon Society, Rebel Slave Communities in the Americas, The John Hopkins University Press, Baltimore, 1979

GLOSSARY

Page 52: Calabash is a food container made from the hard shell of a gourd. The premature gourd is picked off the tree when its shell is green and pliable. All its seeds and inner contents are discarded, before the shell is carved with artistic images and left in the sun to dry.

Page 58: "Blue foot come from yonder." The term refers to people who migrated from other parts of the island of Jamaica to live in the district.